# The Collins Book of
# FAIRY TALES

*Illustrated by*
CAROLINE SHARPE

COLLINS

ACKNOWLEDGEMENTS

General Editor Anne Scott
Design by Enid Fairhead

*Adaptations of traditional stories by*

| | |
|---|---|
| SUSAN DICKINSON | INGRID SELBERG |
| JANE FIOR | CAROLINE STENNING |
| EMILY GIBSON | BOBBIE WHITCOMBE |
| SOPHIE GIBSON | DIANE WILMER |
| ANNE SCOTT | LESLEY YOUNG |

ISBN 0 00 195218 8

First published 1983
Copyright © Text and illustrations
William Collins Sons & Co Ltd 1983
Made and printed in Great Britain by
William Collins Sons & Co Ltd Glasgow

# The Collins Book of
# FAIRY TALES

# Contents

# Jack and the Beanstalk

"Tomorrow you must take our cow to the market," said Jack's mother one day. "There is scarcely a crust left for us to eat, and the cow is the only thing we have to sell. See you get a good price for it; otherwise we shall surely starve."

Jack loved the little cow and a few tears trickled down his cheeks as he led it along the dusty road early next morning.

"Why so sad, young fellow?" a voice said.

Jack, who had seen no one approach him, jumped in surprise. A strange little man dressed all in green stood before him.

"I'm t-t-taking our cow to sell at the m-m-market," Jack stuttered, "f-f-for we have no money left to buy f-f-food."

"It's a long way to the town," said the stranger. "Sell the cow to me instead."

"Will you give me a good price?" asked Jack.

"I will give you this bag of beans. They are magic beans and you will not be sorry that you have given me your cow," said the little man.

So Jack took the bag of beans and raced back to his mother's cottage to tell her what a good bargain he had made.

"A bag of beans for a good cow!" his mother cried angrily. "You stupid boy. Now we shall surely starve." She boxed Jack's ears and threw the beans out of the window.

That night Jack went hungry to bed, wishing he had never met the strange little man on the road to the market.

He rose early next morning, planning to go into the woods to gather berries. But when he let himself out of the cottage, he got the biggest surprise of his life. In the little patch of garden an enormously tall tree had grown in the night.

"The magic beans," Jack whispered to himself. "A giant beanstalk has sprung up on the spot where Mother threw the beans!"

The beanstalk was so tall that Jack could not see the top. He started to climb. Up and up he went till he was as high as the clouds, but still he had not reached the top. Resting for a moment Jack then climbed on until at last the beanstalk stopped and Jack stepped onto a wondrous land in the sky where everything was blue – trees, flowers, birds, fields. Close by stood an enormous blue castle.

"Perhaps I can get something to eat," thought hungry Jack, as he set off towards the castle.

He had to use both hands to lift the heavy knocker on the great blue door, and when he let it go a loud boom echoed through the castle.

5

Almost at once the door opened and there stood a giantess grasping a rolling-pin in one hand.

"P-please may I have a crust to eat?" Jack's voice wobbled with fright.

"My husband, the giant will have *you* to eat if he finds you here, little boy," the giantess answered. But she had quite a kind heart and gave Jack an enormous slice of bread and cheese.

Suddenly there was a great roar.

"Quickly, it's my husband. Into the oven with you," cried the giantess.

Next moment a huge, ugly giant strode into the kitchen. Two sheep dangled from his belt. The giant sniffed the air.

"Fee-fi-fo-fum,

I smell the blood of an Englishman,

Be he alive, or be he dead

I'll have his bones to grind my bread," he bellowed.

"Nonsense," said his wife. "It is only your breakfast you smell." And she placed before him a great pie as big as a door.

When the giant had eaten, he lay back in his chair and called out. "Bring me my money bags, wife. I shall count my gold."

Clink, clink, clink, went the coins, until the giant grew sleepy and his eyes began to close. This was Jack's chance to escape.

6

Quiet as a mouse he crept out of the oven, and snatching up a bag of gold coins, he fled. He was half way down the beanstalk before the giant awoke.

"Mother, we'll never be poor again," Jack cried, showing her the bag of gold.

But the gold did not last forever and one morning Jack again climbed the beanstalk.

Everything happened as before and again Jack was hiding in the oven.

"Bring me my magic hen," the giant bellowed, after eating an enormous breakfast.

When his wife put it on the table in front of him, he cried, "Lay!" and the hen laid an egg of gold. Again he cried, "Lay!" and the hen laid another egg of gold.

At last the giant's eyes began to close and soon his snores filled the whole castle.

Quickly and silently Jack crept out of the oven, snatched up the magic hen and fled. The hen cackled loudly, but Jack was at the foot of the beanstalk before the ogre had rubbed the sleep from his eyes.

*Now* Jack and his mother would never be poor again. All they had to say was "Lay!" and the magic hen laid an egg of gold.

Jack climbed the beanstalk only once more. This time he hid behind a bush in the giant's garden. Through the kitchen window he heard the giant call for his magic harp and soon the castle was filled with beautiful music.

"My mother would love that harp," said Jack to himself, and waiting only for the giant to fall asleep, he climbed through the window, snatched up the harp and was off like the wind.

But the harp gave a loud twang and this time the giant was on his feet in an instant. Roaring with rage, he raced after Jack.

Jack was half way down the beanstalk when it began to shake violently. The ogre was coming down after him. Jack yelled with all his might to his mother. "Bring an axe; quickly, bring an axe!"

Next moment he had jumped the last few feet, seized the axe from his frightened mother and with a few mighty chops, cut the beanstalk in two.

Down came the beanstalk and down came the giant – with such a thud that he vanished from sight into the earth, never to be seen again.

And Jack and his mother were rich and happy for the rest of their lives.

# The Three Little Pigs

There were once three little pigs who decided it was time to leave home and set up house for themselves. So they wished each other good luck and went their separate ways.

The first little pig came across a bale of straw that no one seemed to want. He set to and made himself a fine straw house with a tuft on top. He was sitting inside admiring his little house when he heard a wolf outside calling, "Little pig, little pig, let me come in."

But the pig answered, "No, no, not by the hair on my chinny chin chin."

The wolf smacked his lips and said, "Then I'll huff and I'll puff and I'll blow your house down."

And he huffed and he puffed and he blew the straw house down, and the little pig was gobbled up.

The second little pig was passing through a forest when he came across a large bundle of twigs that someone had left. In a clearing in the forest he made himself a fine cone-shaped house of twigs, a bit like a wigwam. He was sitting inside resting his trotters when he heard the wolf at the door calling, "Little pig, little pig, let me come in."

But the pig answered, "No, no, not by the hair on my chinny chin chin."

The wolf drew in his breath and said, "Then I'll huff and I'll puff and I'll blow your house down."

And he huffed and he puffed and he blew the twig house down, and the little pig was gobbled up.

The third little pig came across a load of bricks that had fallen off a lorry. He spent a long time building himself a solid house of bricks with a fine chimney. He was sitting inside roasting an apple when he heard the wolf at the door calling, "Little pig, little pig, let me come in."

But the pig answered, "No, no, not by the hair on my chinny chin chin."

The wolf drew himself up to his full height and said, "Then I'll huff and I'll puff and I'll blow your house down."

And he huffed and he puffed, but he could not blow the brick house down.

When he was quite out of breath, he said, "Little pig, I know where there is a fine field of turnips."

"Really, where?" asked the little pig.

"At Farmer Barleycorn's", replied the wolf. "I'll call for you at seven o'clock tomorrow morning and we'll go along together."

"I'll be ready," said the little pig.

But the next morning the little pig got up at six o'clock, went to Farmer Barleycorn's, and was home again with a load of turnips before the wolf was even up.

When the wolf found out he had been tricked, he came back and

called to the little pig, "Little pig, I know where there's an apple tree covered in juicy apples."

"Is that so? Where?" asked the little pig.

"In the mayor's garden," said the wolf. "Meet me there at six o'clock tomorrow morning."

"I'll be there," said the little pig.

But the next morning the little pig got up at five o'clock and took his basket off to the mayor's garden. He had filled it and was home again making an apple dumpling before the wolf was even up.

The wolf was growing more and more angry. The next day he again called on the little pig and said, "Little pig, a fair is coming to town this afternoon. Shall we go? I'll call for you at three."

"I'll be waiting," said the little pig.

But once more the little pig went along early. He won a fine butter churn at the coconut shy and was going home with it when he saw the wolf at the bottom of a hill. Quick as a flash the little pig got inside the churn and rolled down the hill at great speed towards the wolf. The wolf was terrified and raced off home, his tail between his legs.

The wolf decided that enough was enough. He was going to have the little pig for his supper that very night.

He went to the little pig's house and climbed onto the roof. Of course! The chimney! It was wide enough for him to slither down!

The little pig heard the wolf's paws padding about on the roof above his head. Quickly he put his huge pot of boiling stock on the fire. Just at that moment the wolf came down the chimney in a great rush and landed *Splash*! in the pot. The little pig put the lid on top and cried, "Hurrah! Wolf stew for supper!"

That evening he was able to sit down to a fine meal, undisturbed by any knocks at the door.

# Cinderella

There once was a beautiful young girl called Cinderella who lived with her ugly stepmother and her two ugly stepsisters. And because they were ugly they hated Cinderella and made her life very unhappy. Day after day she had to wash, scrub, sweep and stitch, and night after night poor tired Cinderella would crouch by the dying embers of the kitchen fire and weep.

Then one day the king of the land announced that his son, the prince, would choose a wife at a Grand Ball to be given at the palace. Every young lady from far and near was invited.

"I should like to go to the ball too," sighed Cinderella, as she stitched rich satin into ball gowns for her ugly stepsisters.

"You go to the ball!" her stepmother laughed harshly. "Dressed in your rags covered with ashes from the kitchen fire?"

And Cinderella wept.

The night of the ball came. Sadly Cinderella helped the ugly sisters to dress, tied bows and buttons, smoothed folds, brushed their hair. Ready at last, their mother swept her daughters to the waiting carriage. And Cinderella sat down as usual by the kitchen fire and wished and wished that she might meet the prince.

"Why do you sit there so sadly?" said a gentle voice. "You should be at the ball."

Cinderella looked up and blinked in astonishment. A little lady in a red cloak stood before her. In one hand she held a wand which glowed like a tiny green fire.

"I am your fairy godmother," she said, tapping Cinderella lightly on the shoulder with her wand.

In an instant Cinderella's rags vanished and she wore a gown of purest white glittering with emeralds. Glass slippers shone on her feet.

"Now you *will* go to the ball," said the fairy godmother.

"But how am I to get to the palace?" Cinderella asked.

"Help me to carry that pumpkin into the garden," said the little lady. Then at one tap of her wand, the pumpkin became a splendid glass coach. At a second tap, six little fieldmice were turned into six handsome white horses.

"Off to the ball with you," said the fairy godmother. "But remember you must leave the palace as the clock strikes twelve."

Joyfully Cinderella promised. "And thank you for making my wish come true," she said.

At the palace, the ballroom was ablaze with light, and as the beautiful Cinderella stood in the doorway all heads turned towards her in wonder. At once the prince asked her to dance and Cinderella's eyes shone with happiness.

All evening the prince danced only with her.

"Will you be my princess?" he whispered to Cinderella. But just at that moment, the palace clock began to strike. It was midnight.

Like the wind Cinderella sped from the ballroom, but in her flight she left one glass slipper behind on the palace steps.

When her stepmother and stepsisters returned from the ball, Cinderella was sitting as usual in her rags by the dying embers of the fire.

At the palace the prince picked up the glass slipper, vowing that its owner would be his wife.

For six days the prince's heralds travelled the land with the lost glass slipper. Every girl tried to make it fit her foot. On the seventh day a herald arrived at Cinderella's house. The ugly sisters tried on the glass slipper, but no matter how they pushed and pulled, it was too short for one and too narrow for the other. In their anger, they looked uglier than ever.

"Is there no one else in this house?" asked the herald.

"Only Cinderella," her stepmother laughed. "But she is little more than a servant and was certainly not at the ball."

"Let her try on the slipper," the herald answered.

And Cinderella slipped it onto her foot and it fitted perfectly. With a little smile she took the other glass slipper from the pocket of her ragged apron.

So the happy prince found his princess and in the whole kingdom only three people did not rejoice – Cinderella's stepmother and her ugly daughters.

# Lazy Jack

Once upon a time there was a boy named Jack. He lived with his mother in a small cottage on a common. They were very poor and Jack's mother earned her living by spinning. But Jack was very lazy and in summer did nothing but bask in the sun and in winter sit by the hearth. He was therefore nicknamed Lazy Jack.

One day his mother could stand it no longer and told him that if he did not begin to work for his food she would turn him out and he would have to earn his living as best he could.

So the next day Jack went out and hired himself to a neighbouring farmer for a penny. But when he was coming home, as he had never had any money before, he lost the penny while crossing a brook.

His mother was very angry and told him he should have put it in his pocket.

"I'll do that next time," answered Jack.

The next day the farmer told Jack that for a day's work he would give him a jar of milk. Jack took the jar and tried to squeeze it into the pocket of his jacket, spilling all the milk long before he reached home.

"You stupid boy!" shouted his mother. "You should have carried it on your head."

"I'll do that next time," Jack replied.

The following day the farmer agreed to give Jack some butter for his labours. In the evening he took the butter and put it on his head. It had been a hot day and the butter melted and when Jack got home his hair was full of it.

"You stupid lout!" his mother shouted. "You should have carried it in your hand."

"I'll remember that next time," said Jack.

The next day the farmer gave Jack a puppy for his services. On the
way home Jack carried the puppy in his hand, but after a while the
puppy began to struggle and Jack was forced to let go.

His mother was very upset. "You should have tied it with a string
and pulled it along behind you," she said.

"I'll do that next time," answered Jack.

The next day after his work the farmer rewarded Jack with a shoulder
of lamb. Jack tied some string round the lamb and dragged it along
behind him. When he reached home the meat was absolutely ruined.

"You nincompoop!" yelled his mother. "That meat should have
been carried on your shoulder."

"All right, Mother. I'll do that another time," replied Jack.

The following day the farmer was very pleased with Jack and gave
him a donkey. Jack remembered what his mother had said and hoisted
the donkey onto his shoulder. On his way home Jack passed the house
of a wealthy merchant who had a beautiful daughter. Unfortunately
she was unable to speak, and doctors had said that she would never be
able to speak unless someone, or something made her laugh. As it
happened she was just looking out of the window when Jack walked
by with the donkey on his shoulder. This was such a comical sight
that she burst out laughing and immediately her speech was restored.

Her father was so happy that he summoned Jack and said that he
would make him a rich gentleman and his mother a rich woman if
Jack would agree to marry his daughter. Jack was overjoyed and the
marriage promptly took place. The couple then lived in a large house
in great happiness.

# The Frog Prince

A princess once had a golden ball. It was her favourite toy and she loved to take it into the woods where in a green glade beside a spring she played with it all day long. But one summer day as she was tossing the ball into the air and catching it again, it slipped out of her hands and rolled towards the spring and fell in. The princess looked into the water and could see her ball gleaming way way down.

Her beautiful ball was gone for ever! The princess burst into tears.

Suddenly she heard a voice say: "What is the trouble, Princess?"

She looked all round and saw a green frog on the edge of the spring looking at her with his froggy eyes. "Oh," she said, "my lovely golden ball has fallen into the water and I'll never get it out again. And how shall I tell my father?"

"If I dive down and fetch it for you, will you let me be your playmate, sit at your table, eat off your plate, sleep in your bed?"

"Yes, yes, anything you like," said the princess.

The frog swam down to the bottom of the spring and brought the ball up in his mouth. He tossed it on the ground at the princess's feet. Picking it up, she ran off gaily back to the palace, never heeding the frog's cries of "Wait for me! Wait for me!"

At dinner that evening there was a gentle knocking at the great door of the dining hall and a voice called:

"Princess, Princess, let me in." The princess got up from her place and opened the door, but when she saw the frog outside she shut it again quickly. The king inquired who was there, and the princess told him how the frog had brought back her ball on condition she let him sit beside her and eat off her plate and sleep in her bed.

"If you made a promise, you must keep it," said the king. "Let the frog in at once."

So the princess opened the door and the frog hopped across the room and up onto the princess's chair and then onto the white tablecloth. "Push your plate nearer so I may eat," he said.

The princess shuddered and pushed her golden plate near him. The frog ate a hearty dinner, but the princess couldn't touch a thing.

"Now I am tired," said the frog. "Let us go to bed." The princess looked at her father and begged him to put the frog out into the garden, but the king insisted she take the frog upstairs with her.

Holding the frog between her finger and thumb, the princess climbed the stairs to her bedchamber.

"Put me on your pillow beside you," ordered the frog. She couldn't bear to do that, so she dropped him in a corner of the room, while she prepared for bed. But no sooner had she climbed between the silken sheets than the frog hopped up onto the pillow.

The princess lay as far away from him as she could and at last she fell asleep.

In the morning, to her joy, the frog had vanished. But great was her surprise when a handsome prince approached and kissed her.

"Dear Princess," he said. "You have released me from the wicked fairy's spell. Unless a princess let me eat from her plate and sleep in her bed I was condemned to remain a frog for the rest of my life. But now I am free, will you marry me and be my queen?"

And that's exactly what happened. The next day the prince and princess drove off in a fine coach to his father's kingdom where they married and lived in great happiness.

# Mr Vinegar

Poor Mr Vinegar lived with his wife, his cat and his canary in a vinegar bottle. One day, tidy Mrs Vinegar swept the floor so fiercely that she knocked the broom-handle right through the bottle. Shaking glass out of her hair, she ran off to find her husband.

"Oh," she cried. "I've smashed our home with that clumsy broom!"

"Oh," said Mr Vinegar when he saw the damage. "But we still have the wooden door." He heaved it onto his back. "Fetch the cat and the canary and let us go and seek our fortune!"

So they set out and trudged on and on till night fell.

"If we haul this door into a tree, we can sleep on it," said Mr Vinegar.

"What a good idea," said Mrs Vinegar. And soon they were fast asleep

in an old oak tree. Suddenly they were jerked awake by harsh voices and the clink of coins. There were three robbers at the foot of their tree.

Mr and Mrs Vinegar were terrified. They trembled so much that they shook the door and themselves down onto the robbers. Then it was the robbers who were terrified. They took to their heels and fled.

When the sun came up Mr and Mrs Vinegar found themselves sitting on a pile of golden guineas.

"We're rich," cried Mr Vinegar, when he had counted up to forty.

"I shall look for somewhere to live," said his wife. "You must take these forty guineas to the next town, and buy a cow. Then I can make butter and cheese to sell, and we shall live quite well."

Mr Vinegar soon found someone at the market with a cow to sell. It was a lovely golden red.

"I'll give you forty guineas for your beautiful cow," said Mr Vinegar to the owner.

"She's yours!" said the man quickly, knowing it was too much to pay.

As he was leading the cow through the busy town, Mr Vinegar saw a man playing a bagpipe. He was taking pocketfuls of money from the crowd.

"There's a quicker way to make a fortune," muttered Mr Vinegar. And to the piper he said, "'Tis a wonderful instrument."

"'Tis, 'tis. And pays the player too," said the man.

"What would you take for it?" inquired Mr Vinegar. "All I have is this cow."

"That'll do," said the piper, quickly handing over his bagpipe.

Mr Vinegar tried to play a tune, but the pipe just squealed and wailed. People shouted, boys threw stones, and Mr Vinegar knew it was time to leave town. Besides, a cold wind was turning his fingers blue. Then he saw a man coming along wearing a pair of thick leather gloves.

"This bagpipe for your thick leather gloves!" Mr Vinegar offered.

"Done!" said the man. And next moment gloves and bagpipe had changed hands.

But Mr Vinegar was getting tired, so when he saw a man striding along with a fine stout stick, he gladly gave up his leather gloves for it.

Back at the old oak tree a wise old crow perched on a branch.

"You spent all your money on a cow," he croaked, "exchanged her for a bagpipe you could not play, exchanged the pipe for a pair of old gloves and even gave *them* away for a stick you could have cut from any hedge! Foolish Mr Vinegar! Caw, Caw!" Mr Vinegar was so cross that he flung the stick at the crow and it was lost among the branches. So foolish Mr Vinegar had nothing at all to take back to his wife. She *was* angry!

# The Princess and the Pea

Once upon a time there lived a handsome prince. He was as kind as he was brave and his mother doted on him. Nothing was ever too much trouble, for one day he would be king of the land.

When he was eighteen, it was time for his parents to find him a bride. And because of his royal blood, it wasn't enough to find a beautiful and pleasing girl, she had to be a princess too. So messengers were sent far and wide to seek out suitable princesses.

The prince, who was not sure that he wanted to marry at all, was alarmed to hear how many young women were expected to visit the palace in the hope of being chosen.

"Do I have to see them all?" he asked his mother in dismay. "And how do you know that they are princesses?"

"Don't worry, my son. There is one sure way of telling whether a person is of royal blood. I shall test each one before we make a decision."

The prince sighed and went back to the stables to ride his favourite horse while the queen bustled off to attend to the arrangements. First she ordered the bed to be made up in the visitor's bedchamber. The maids were asked to place ten feather mattresses one on top of the other, and cover them with silk sheets and a swansdown coverlet. Next the palace carpenter was told to construct a special pair of steps, for the bed was now so high that it was impossible to climb into it in the normal way. When everything was ready, the queen secretly slipped a pea under the mattresses.

That evening, the first of the princesses arrived. After she had dined with the royal family, the queen took her up to the bedchamber and bid her goodnight. Next morning when she came down to breakfast, the queen asked her how she had slept.

"Like a top," replied the young woman, yawning and stretching.

"I see," said the queen icily. "That will be all. You may leave."

The prince was mystified as one after another, young women were entertained royally only to be dismissed as unsuitable next morning. When he asked his mother to explain, she just said that not one was good enough for him. And they were certainly not princesses.

20

By the time one hundred young women had visited the palace, the prince suggested that it might be best to postpone the idea of a marriage and to his relief, his parents agreed.

That night, there was a great storm. As the king and the queen and the prince sat down to eat, a manservant hurried to the king and whispered something in his ear.

"My dear," said the king, "a young woman has just presented herself at the gate. She says that she's a princess but evidently she looks more like a servant girl."

"Lay her a place," said the queen, "and bring her in."

The prince looked up in surprise as a young girl was shown into the room. She came over and sat shyly beside him. Her dress was in tatters and covered in mud, but she had a sweet face and he enjoyed talking to her. When they had all finished eating, his mother took the girl upstairs to bed. The prince was sad to think that he would not be allowed to marry her because she was the first girl he had really liked.

The next morning he was sitting at the breakfast table with his parents when the young girl came down. She looked exhausted.

"How did you sleep?" asked the queen.

"Forgive me, Ma'am," said the girl, "I don't know why, but I could not sleep a wink. I tossed and turned all night long and when I got up this morning, I found that I was covered in bruises."

"Hurrah!" cried the queen, much to the prince's surprise. She turned to the king. "Did you hear, my dear? Couldn't sleep and she's covered in bruises! My son, at last we've found a bride worthy of you."

"I'm very glad that you've chosen her," said the prince, "but tell me, how did you know that she was the one?"

"Easy!" said the queen. "Only a real princess could have been so inconvenienced by the presence of a pea!"

# Hansel and Gretel

Once upon a time there was a poor woodcutter and he lived with his wife and his two children, Hansel and Gretel, at the edge of a very large forest. Times were hard and food was scarce. The woodcutter did his best but his family often went to bed hungry.

One night as the children lay in their beds, they heard their stepmother say, "Husband, there's four mouths to feed but I've only food left for two. Tomorrow we must take Hansel and Gretel out into the forest and leave them there."

"Wife," said their father in horror, "we'll do no such thing. What will become of them, alone, without shelter?"

"If you don't agree, we'll all starve," replied the stepmother angrily, and the children listened as she persuaded their father to do as she bid. Gretel was frightened and began to cry.

"Shhh," whispered Hansel. "Dry your eyes. I have a plan."

He waited until his parents were safely asleep, then he tiptoed out into the forest. It was a cold, clear night and the moon shone brightly through the trees down onto the earth, where white pebbles lay gleaming. Hansel filled his pockets with pebbles and crept back to bed.

"Go to sleep now, Gretel," he said. "All will be well."

The following morning, the stepmother woke the children up early. "Get up," she said, giving them each a shake. "We are going to spend the day in the forest gathering wood. Here is a crust of bread for midday. Don't lose it, for it's all you'll get."

The woodcutter and his wife walked deep into the forest, followed by Hansel and Gretel. Gretel did her best to keep up, but Hansel dawdled behind.

"Hurry up, Hansel," said his father. "Why are you walking so slowly?"

"I am looking at my white dove. It is sitting on the roof of the house and saying goodbye to me."

"Stuff and nonsense," said the stepmother. "That's no dove. That's just the morning sun shining on the chimney." But Hansel still walked slowly, secretly scattering pebbles one by one along the path.

Finally the stepmother stopped. "Wait here, dear children," she said. "Your father and I are going to chop down some wood. We'll come back to fetch you later."

The children rested on a pile of leaves and soon fell asleep. When

they awoke, it was night. The leaves shivered as the wind blew the branches of the trees, and the moon was shining.

Gretel was frightened and clung to her brother, as an owl screeched and fluttered its wings in the tree above.

"Look!" cried Hansel. He pointed to the path where the trail of white pebbles beckoned the children towards home. How quickly they ran back through the forest.

"Father, Father!" the children called, as they ran in through the door. "Wake up! We are safe, we are home!"

Their father was overjoyed to see them, but their stepmother snapped, "Where did you get to? We were worried that we'd lost you."

For a little while, things were easier. Then one evening, just as he was about to go to sleep, Hansel heard his stepmother say to his father, "Husband, the larder is empty again. We must take the children into the forest, and this time they must not find their way back."

Hansel waited until his parents were asleep, but when he tried to go out and collect pebbles, he found the door bolted and barred.

The next morning the children were woken early. Each was given a crust of bread, and following their father, they set off down the forest path.

"Hurry up, Hansel," said the stepmother irritably, as Hansel dawdled along the way. "What are you doing?"

"I'm looking at my pet dove. It is sitting on the roof of the house and saying goodbye to me."

"Stuff and nonsense," said the stepmother. "That's no dove. That's just the morning sun shining on the chimney."

But Hansel continued to loiter, and as he walked, he broke his bread and scattered the tiny white crumbs in a trail behind him.

The family went far, far into the forest until at last the stepmother said, "Lie down, dear children, and rest. We'll be back by and by."

So Hansel and Gretel lay down and were soon fast asleep.

When they awoke, it was late. The moon shone down, but there were no little crumbs to guide them home. The birds had eaten every one.

23

Gretel looked at Hansel in fright, but he said, "Don't worry, Gretel. We'll soon find our way home."

So, hand in hand, the two children made their way through the dark forest. Suddenly, Gretel stopped and sniffed the air. "I can smell smoke," she said. "Maybe there's a cottage nearby." And sure enough, the path forked and there ahead, in a mossy glade, stood a dear little house. There was no sign of the owner, and the children crept up to peep through the window. As Hansel put his face close to the glass, he smelled the sweet smell of barley sugar, and as Gretel stooped to peep through the keyhole, she saw that the door was made of chocolate. The whole house was made of biscuits and candy! The children were so hungry that they started to tear at the walls. And they were so busy eating, that they did not see the door open and an old woman hobble out. "Children! What are you doing?" she shouted.

Hansel explained what had happened.

The old woman seemed concerned. "Come in, children, and make yourselves at home," she crooned. "How thin you both are. Stay with me for a while and I'll soon fatten you up." And she showed them to a little bedroom with two feather-beds and did all she could to make them feel comfortable.

Hansel and Gretel enjoyed staying with the old woman. She fed them with sweetmeats and in no time at all they were healthy and plump.

One morning Gretel woke up and found Hansel's bed empty. She ran downstairs and said to the old woman, "Where's Hansel?"

The old witch, for that's what she was, turned and said unpleasantly, "Never mind where he is. It's time you started to work for your keep. Out you go and gather me sticks. I'm going to light my oven."

Gretel went down to the woodpile and on her way, she heard Hansel's voice calling. "Gretel," he whispered. "The old woman has

24

tied me up and put me in the henhouse. Do what she tells you, but mind you take care."

Gretel spent the day carrying wood to the kitchen, wondering how she could set Hansel free. The old witch lit a roaring fire in the oven and told Gretel to lay the table for supper.

"Gretel," she called. "Do you think the oven is ready? Come and put your head inside and see if it is hot enough."

Gretel thought of poor Hansel and she replied, "Gladly. But I'm not sure how to do it. Will you show me first?"

"Stupid girl," scolded the old witch. "Just put your head inside like this." And she opened the oven door.

Quick as lightning, Gretel gave her a shove and the wicked witch fell head first into the oven. Gretel slammed the door to, and bolted it firmly. Then she ran down the path and let Hansel out of the henhouse and the two children threw their arms around each other.

There was a flapping of wings, and there perched in a fir tree was Hansel's white dove. The bird flew a little way along the path and waited until the children caught up with him.

"Come, Gretel," called Hansel happily. "My dove will guide us home!"

It was dark when they reached the woodcutter's cottage. They pushed the door open and saw their father sitting in his chair, staring sadly into the empty grate.

"Father! We're safe. We're home!" cried Hansel and Gretel.

The woodcutter jumped up and ran to hug them. "Children!" he cried, tears running down his cheeks. "I thought I'd never see you again. Your stepmother has left. From now on, we'll never be parted."

Hansel and Gretel worked hard to help their father, and although they were always poor, they were never hungry. The little family lived quietly and happily on the edge of the forest, and the stepmother never came back.

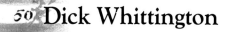

## 50 Dick Whittington

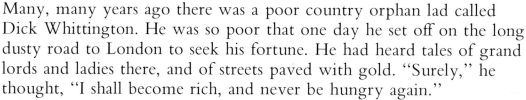

Many, many years ago there was a poor country orphan lad called Dick Whittington. He was so poor that one day he set off on the long dusty road to London to seek his fortune. He had heard tales of grand lords and ladies there, and of streets paved with gold. "Surely," he thought, "I shall become rich, and never be hungry again."

But when he reached London, he found no streets of gold, only grey cobbles. The people, too, were grey-faced, and either too haughty or too busy to notice a tired, ragged boy. For two days Dick searched for work, and for two nights he huddled in doorways, cold and hungry.

"I shall go home to my own village," said Dick to himself on the third morning. "At least people are friendly there even though they are poor."

Wearily, he trudged up the long hill out of the city. As he rested against a milestone, he could hear the church bells in the distance. They seemed to be saying,

> *Turn again, Whittington,*
> *Thrice Lord Mayor of London.*

"Lord Mayor!" cried Dick. "Me? Surely not." But he *did* turn, hopeful once more, and went back to the city.

The next morning, he was hauled off his doorstep by an angry cook.

"Get up, you rascal!" she shouted. "Lazing about in honest folks' doorways! Off with you, or I'll find work for you to do!"

"Please," said Dick, "I should be glad to work for some breakfast."

And so Dick became a kitchen-boy. He cleaned pots and fetched and carried from dawn till dusk, but now he was not hungry, and he had a bed in the attic to sleep in. There were mice in the eaves, but with the first pennies he earned Dick bought a cat, which kept the mice away, and warmed his feet at night.

Sometimes Alice, the little girl of the house, would slip down to the kitchen and talk to him. Dick would tell her of his life in the country, and how he had turned back into London because of the song of the bells.

Now, the master of the house, Mr Fitzwarren, was a merchant, whose ships carried goods to trade in far-away countries. It was his custom when a ship set sail, to let everyone who worked for him send something to sell too. When all the other servants had given him their goods Mr Fitzwarren turned to Dick.

"I have nothing," he said, "but my cat, and I could not part with her."

"You must venture something," said Mr Fitzwarren, "to bring us luck on the voyage."

So, sadly, Dick brought his cat and gave her to the ship's captain.

When the ship reached the coast of Africa, the captain went straight to the palace of a rich sultan. The sultan and all his court were eager to buy his fine wares, and he soon had a pile of gold to take home. But as the captain left the palace he saw everywhere swarms of rats and mice. This gave him an idea.

"Bring Dick Whittington's cat," he said to a sailor.

No sooner was the cat in the palace than ten rats lay dead. Terrified, the rest – and the mice – scuttled to their holes.

"I will give you a thousand gold pieces for this wondrous animal," cried the delighted sultan.

"She has been a good friend to us, and an excellent ship's cat," murmured the captain.

"Five thousand pieces, perhaps? And this jewel?" said the sultan flashing it before the captain's eyes.

And so the ship returned to England without Dick's cat. He was sad to have lost her, but she had made his fortune.

In time, Dick married the golden-haired Alice Fitzwarren and, ten years later, when he was Lord Mayor of London, he remembered the message of the bells:

*Turn again, Whittington,*
*Thrice Lord Mayor of London.*

# Rumpelstiltskin

"My pretty daughter can spin gold out of straw," a boastful miller once said to the king.

"What a gift!" exclaimed the king. "Send her to my castle.

Next morning the king took the miller's daughter to a room filled with straw. "Here is a spinning-wheel," he said. "Spin this straw into gold by dawn, or you will die!" And he banged the door shut.

The poor girl could not really spin gold from straw, and she sat down and cried and cried. Suddenly the door crashed open and a strange little man stepped in.

"Why are you weeping?" he asked.

"Alas! If I cannot spin this straw into gold I shall die," the girl sobbed.

"I will do it for you if you give me something in return," said the little man.

"Will you take my scarf?" she offered.

"Very well," said the little man and he began to spin. He worked all night, and by morning the room was full of spun gold.

The king was delighted. "But I have a bigger room with even more straw in it," he said. "Tonight you will spin that into gold too or you will die."

The girl wept. But the little man came again.

"I will spin gold for —"

"My ring!" cried the girl.

"Very well," the little man agreed.

The greedy king loved the beautiful bright gold, and he wanted still more.

"I shall have the biggest room in the castle filled with straw," he said. "If you spin it all by morning you will be my wife."

Hardly had the girl begun to cry than the little man appeared.

"I have nothing left to give you," she moaned.

"When you become queen, you must give me your first child," said he. And the girl promised, hoping the little man would forget.

So the straw was spun. And the king was satisfied at last.

"You shall be my queen tomorrow," he said.

A year later, a princess was born, and the little man appeared before the queen.

"Take all my jewels," she wept, "but do not take away my child." And she sobbed so long and so loud that the little man took pity on her.

"You have three days to guess my name," he said. "If you get it right, you may keep your baby."

The queen sat up all night thinking of names. Next day, when the little man arrived, she tried them all, from Abercrombie to Zebediah.

"None of those is my name," he cried, and danced a little jig. Next day the queen sent messengers all over the country to collect names. "Are you called Bandylegs, Wurzelhead, or Snout?" she asked. "Duckfoot, Goldfingers, or Greedie-Meanie?" And she tried lots more.

But the little man said: "No . . . . no . . . . no!" to them all. And his smile showed all his sharp teeth.

On the third day, a messenger came to the queen and said, "Deep in the forest, by a tiny house, I saw a little man dancing round a fire. He was singing this song:

> *'I'll name you, says she.*
> *Oh no, you won't, says me,*
> *For never was there ever*
> *Anyone so clever*
> *As Rumpelstiltskin!' "*

"Well done, my baby is saved. Take the rest of the day off," cried the queen joyfully. She could hardly wait for the horrible little man to arrive.

"You're called Frogwhistle," she declared.

"No I'm not," said the little man.

"Spoonplacket-Tarpot?"

"That's silly."

"What about Rumpelstiltskin, then?"

The terrible little man jumped up and down with rage.

"A witch told you!" he shrieked. "Aa-aa-aa-AH!!" He stamped his left foot so hard that he toppled over. And, catching hold of his right foot to save himself from falling, he split right up the middle. And that was the end of Rumpelstiltskin.

# Four Red Caps

Willie was a ship's carpenter who lived in the village of Kintail in Scotland. One day he needed a piece of wood to mend a hole in his own boat, so he set out for the forest.

Willie couldn't find exactly what he was looking for and, before he knew it, a mist had come down and the sun was sinking below the trees. Willie knew the forest like his own backyard – and he knew there was no shelter to be found.

Imagine how surprised he was to see a light shining through the trees! Following it, he came to an old hut and knocked at the door. The door creaked open and an old wizened face looked out.

"Can you give me shelter?" asked Willie. "I have lost my way and the mist is as thick as porridge."

"Step inside and I'll ask my sisters," said the old woman.

Two old women were toasting bannocks at a peat fire.

"Look what the wind's blown in," said the first old hag.

"It's a wild night. Let him have our bed – we won't be using it tonight!" cackled her sister.

Gratefully Willie drank some hot tea and ate a bannock before following the old woman to the bedroom, where he was soon asleep.

He was woken by one of the old women rummaging in a chest in the room. As Willie watched, she pulled out a red cap, put it on and cried, "Here's off to London Town!" With a great whoosh she disappeared up the chimney.

Of course, Willie realized with a start! The old women were witches!

Willie watched as the other two old women followed suit – on with a red cap each and whoosh! whoosh! up the chimney with a "Here's off to London Town!"

Leaping out of bed, Willie looked in the chest. One red cap was left. At once he slapped it on his head and called out, "Here's off to London Town!" He found himself lifted up the chimney and, before he could catch his breath, set down in a bright and noisy tavern. Over at a table the three old women sat drinking. Willie joined them.

After a while, the first old woman rose to her feet, put on her red cap and said, "Here's back to Kintail!" Whoosh! and she was gone. Her sisters followed closely behind.

Willie was about to follow, when the serving girl came up and asked for money. None of the old women had paid for their drink, and Willie had drunk a fair bit himself.

"Here's back to Kintail!" he cried, but the red cap was lying on the floor where it had fallen and Willie stayed firmly where he was. He was taken off to the magistrate to explain himself.

"How do you come to be in such a state – and so far from home?" he asked.

"It was all the witches' fault," said Willie. And that was his big mistake.

"Witches! Black magic!" cried the people, and the magistrate said, "To the gallows with him!"

The rope was round Willie's neck. He put his hands in his pockets to stop them trembling – but what was this he felt? The red cap! Someone in the tavern must have stuffed it in his pocket as he left!

"Have you a last wish?" asked the magistrate.

"Let me just put on my old red cap one last time before I die," said Willie.

It was no sooner on his head, than he called out, "Here's back to Kintail!" And he was whooshed up and away.

A moment later he found himself back in his workshop, the gallows plank still at his feet. "That's just the piece of wood I was looking for to mend my boat," said Willie. He took it to the boat at once and it fitted exactly. "It's magic!" said Willie to himself, and it would be a foolish person who would disagree!

# The Fisherman and the Mermaid

A young fisherman sat one day on a rock by the sea. Suddenly he heard a little cry and looking down into a pool below, he saw a beautiful mermaid with tears in her eyes.

"Please carry me to the sea," she wept. "I have missed the tide and soon there will be no water left in this pool. I shall surely die."

The young man was afraid. Sailors had told him that mermaids drew men down to the bottom of the sea with their beauty and they were never seen again. But he was sorry for this little mermaid, and soon the water in the pool would indeed have quite dried up.

"I will carry you to the sea if you promise you will not harm me," he said at last.

"I promise," she answered. And taking a golden comb from her hair, she gave it to the young fisherman. "If you comb the stormy waves with this and call 'Morwenna', the sea will be still. But its magic will last for only nine years."

The young man picked up the mermaid and waded into the sea.

"You may also have three wishes," the mermaid trilled, swimming round him happily. "What will they be?"

"I wish for a new fishing boat," said the young man. "I wish that the fish will swim into my net when I whistle. And I wish that a mermaid's spell will never harm me."

"All this you will have for nine years," the mermaid smiled. Then with a flick of her gleaming tail, she was gone.

The young man waded to the shore. And there on the beach was a brand new fishing boat. It was named *Morwenna*.

The young fisherman became rich. For each time he combed the stormy waves with the mermaid's golden comb, the sea was still. And each time he whistled, a shoal of fish swam into his net. But he was not happy. The young man had fallen in love with the beautiful mermaid and longed to see her again.

And so the nine years passed.

I shall take out my boat just one more time," the young fisherman said to himself. "I shall fish close to the shore, and if I should lose the boat I can swim back easily."

He whistled, but no fish came to his net. He sailed out further and again he whistled. Again no fish came. Again and again he tried, but the magic had gone. By then he was far, far from the shore.

Suddenly his net grew heavy and joyfully he pulled it in. Caught in the net was the beautiful mermaid.

"Nine years have passed since last we met," she smiled. "Come now and be happy at last in my cave at the bottom of the sea."

Gladly the young man took the mermaid's hand and slipped with her into the sea.

One day a large ship put down its anchor at that very spot. The captain was resting near the rail when he heard a little cry. Looking into the water below, he saw a beautiful mermaid with tears in her eyes.

"Please, Captain," she cried. "Will you move your ship. We and our babies cannot easily get in and out of our cave, for your anchor chain lies across it."

The captain pulled up his anchor at once and sailed away. He had heard stories of mermaids who drew men down to the bottom of the sea with their beauty.

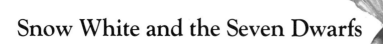

# Snow White and the Seven Dwarfs

Many years ago a young king and queen had a lovely baby daughter. Her skin was as white as snow, her lips as red as blood and her hair as black as jet. They called her Snow White.

But after a few years the young queen died and when the king married again the new queen was very beautiful, but very proud. She had a magic mirror and she would stand before it and say,

"Mirror, mirror on the wall,
Who is the fairest of us all?"
And the mirror would reply,

"Over land and over sea,
None is fairer, Queen, than thee."
But as Snow White grew older, she grew more and more lovely, and one day when the queen stood before her magic mirror and asked,

"Mirror, mirror on the wall,
Who is the fairest of us all?"
the mirror answered:

"Fair indeed, oh Queen, are you,
But Snow White is fairer far, 'tis true."
The queen turned white, then green, with envy and jealousy, and decided that Snow White must die. She summoned a hunter and told him to take Snow White out into the woods and kill her.

The hunter led Snow White deep among the trees, but when he drew his knife to kill her he couldn't bear to do such a terrible deed. So he told her to run far into the forest and never again return to the castle.

Snow White wandered all day, and when it was nearly dark she came to a little cottage. She knocked at the door, but nobody answered, so she lifted the latch, and went in. There she found a fire burning low, and a table set with seven plates, seven goblets and seven napkins. Beside the wall were seven little beds covered with patchwork quilts.

Snow White took a bite of bread and a sip of wine and then she lay down on one of the beds and fell sound asleep.

Not long afterwards the owners of the cottage returned. They were seven dwarfs who dug for gold in the mountains. In they came and took off their boots.

They realized at once that everything was not as they had left it, and looked all round the cottage.

Suddenly one of them shouted: "Who's this sleeping in my bed?"

All the others rushed across the room and gazed at Snow White sleeping soundly under the patchwork quilt.

"How beautiful she is!" they exclaimed.

Snow White opened her eyes and looked at the seven little men. She was rather frightened, but they spoke gently to her and soon she had told them her story.

"You must never return to the castle," they said. "If you would like to keep house for us while we dig for gold in the mountains, we would be delighted. But you must not open the door to anyone. Your wicked stepmother will one day find out where you are and come in search of you."

Now the queen thought that Snow White was dead and did not trouble to go to her magic mirror. But one day she stood in front of it and asked the magic question.

And the mirror answered:

> "Fair indeed, oh Queen, are you,
> But Snow White in a forest dell
> With the seven dwarfs doth dwell,
> And she is fairer far, 'tis true."

Then the queen knew that the huntsman had disobeyed her orders. Staining her face brown and dressing herself in rags so that she looked like an old pedlar woman, she left the castle and went deep into the forest until she came to the cottage of the seven dwarfs. She knocked at the door and called, "Fine wares to sell, fine wares to sell."

Snow White put her head out of the window.

"Pretty trinkets and fine laces for your waist," said the queen, holding up a length of scarlet silk.

Snow White opened the door and let the queen into the cottage.

"Good gracious, child," said the queen, "how badly your dress is laced. Let me do it for you with this scarlet silk."

Snow White stood quite still while her stepmother quickly threaded the lace, but the queen pulled the lace tighter and tighter until Snow White could no longer breathe and she collapsed on the floor.

"That's the end of you and your beauty!" cried the queen as she left the cottage.

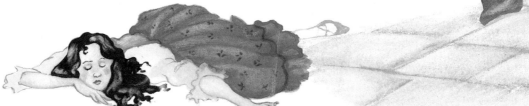

When the dwarfs came home in the evening they found Snow White lying still on the floor. One of them quickly cut the scarlet lace with his knife. Snow White gave a deep sigh and began to breathe again.

"We warned you to let no one in," they said. "Surely it was the wicked queen who was here."

The following morning the queen again asked her mirror,

"Mirror, mirror on the wall,
Who is the fairest of us all?"

When the mirror gave the same answer as before, the queen could hardly believe it, but she knew it was the truth. Snow White must still be alive.

That night the queen went to the orchard and picked an apple. All night long she worked so that one side of the apple was rosy and red, and full of poison, the other side a deep green and quite harmless. Whoever took a bite from the red side was sure to die.

Once again the queen disguised herself and called at the dwarfs' cottage. Once again Snow White looked out of the window when the queen knocked at the door.

"I must not open the door," said Snow White. "The dwarfs have told me not to."

"Very well," said the queen "but let me give you this juicy apple as a present."

"No. I must not," said Snow White.

"Are you afraid it is poisoned?" said the queen. "Here, let us share it." And taking a bite from the green half she handed the apple to Snow White, who bit into the red half.

The next moment Snow White fell to the floor.

"The dwarfs will not be able to save you this time!" cried the queen, and hastened back to the castle.

Once more she stood before her mirror and this time it gave her the answer she wanted:

"Over land and over sea,
None is fairer, Queen, than thee."

When the dwarfs came home they once again found Snow White lying on the floor. But although they loosened the laces at her waist and splashed her with water, she lay quite dead.

"She is so beautiful, we cannot bury her in the black earth," they said. So they made a coffin of glass and placing her in it carried her to the hillside, where one of them watched over her day and night. And all the time she lay there as beautiful as ever.

One day, a king's son rode by and, seeing the coffin with Snow White inside, he asked the dwarfs who she was.

"Give her to me," he begged. But the dwarfs shook their heads.

The prince pleaded with them and at last they agreed, and the prince's servants lifted Snow White in her coffin onto their shoulders. As they did so, one of the servants stumbled and the piece of apple was jolted out of Snow White's mouth. At once she opened her eyes and sat up, alive and well.

The prince was overjoyed and begged her to come with him to his father's castle and be his bride. Snow White gladly consented.

Among the many guests invited to their wedding was Snow White's stepmother. When she was dressed in all her beautiful clothes she stood before her mirror and smiled, sure she would get the answer she wanted.

But the mirror said:

"Fair indeed are you, oh Queen,
But the new bride is the most lovely ever seen."

Raising her hand, the queen smashed the mirror into a thousand pieces. Then she rode off to the wedding to see this beautiful bride. When she arrived at the castle and saw that the bride was Snow White herself, she was transfixed with rage. Her hatred was so great that her heart burst and she fell down dead.

# Three Billy Goats Gruff

In a field beside a river, there lived three handsome billy goats whose name was Gruff. There was Big Billy Goat Gruff, Middle Billy Goat Gruff and Little Billy Goat Gruff.

The field on the other side of the river was covered in much lusher grass than the billy goats' field, and full of tasty buttercups and daisies.

But under the bridge, in a deep pool, lived a wicked old troll. Once, Little Billy Goat Gruff had gone to the edge of the bridge to eat a clump of dandelions, and heard this song come gurgling up:

> *"I'm a troll, fol de rol,*
> *I'm a troll, fol de rol,*
> *I'm a troll, fol de rol,*
> *And I'll eat YOU for my supper. . . ."*

One summer's day, Little Billy Goat Gruff announced, "This is ridiculous! I'm going to tiptoe over that bridge so slowly the old troll won't even hear me."

So, warily, he stepped onto the bridge, trit-trot, trit-trot. But, when he was just halfway across, a loud voice boomed: "Who's that crossing my bridge?"

"It's only me, Little Billy Goat Gruff."

"Is that so?" said the troll. "Well, this is my bridge and I'm going to eat YOU for my supper!"

"Oh no! Don't do that! I'm so small and skinny there's hardly a mouthful on me. But my brother is coming soon. He's much fatter and will make a good supper!"

"All right," said the troll grumpily. "But I hope he's on his way. I'm growing very hungry."

So, trit-trot, trit-trot, Little Billy Goat Gruff went safely on over the bridge and into the field of buttercups and daisies.

At last Middle Billy Goat Gruff thought he too would cross the bridge. But he had no sooner reached the hump in the middle, than he heard a fierce voice bellowing: "Who dares to cross my bridge?"

"It's only me, Middle Billy Goat Gruff – er, Sir."

"Well," said the troll, "this is my bridge and I have been waiting for you to eat you for my supper."

"Oh no! Don't do that! My brother is coming after me. He is such a fine big fellow that he makes me look scrawny."

"Oh, very well," said the troll, "I'm so hungry now I need a good big meal."

So Middle Billy Goat Gruff ran trit-trot down the bridge to the lush pasture, where he settled down to some serious eating.

Big Billy Goat Gruff was lonely. He gazed with longing across the river, where he could see his two brothers eating the flowers all day long. He would have to cross that bridge. He knew there was no point in his trying to tiptoe, so he stepped boldly onto the bridge, clip-clop, clip-clop.

The troll heard Big Billy Goat Gruff's hooves and thought, 'Here's my supper at last.' "Who's that crossing my bridge?" he roared.

"It's me, Big Billy Goat Gruff."

"About time too," grumbled the troll. "I've been waiting all day for you so I'm really hungry and I'm going to eat YOU for my supper!"

And the wicked old troll heaved himself out of his pool and began to climb over the side of the bridge.

"Oh no you don't!" cried Big Billy Goat Gruff. He took a run at the troll and butted him firmly with his sharp horns. The troll toppled backwards and fell into the river with a huge splash!

Then Big Billy Goat Gruff stepped slowly and proudly, clip-clop, clip-clop, down the bridge and into the lush meadow full of flowers, which he began to eat hungrily.

He was so busy eating he didn't notice that his brothers seemed very surprised to see him!

# Cap o'Rushes

A king once had three daughters whom he loved dearly. One day, he called the girls to him and asked them how much they loved him.

"I love you more than I love my life," said one.

"I love you better than anything in the world," said the second.

"I love you as much as uncooked food loves salt," said the third.

"Why, *you* don't love me at all," he said. And he told her to leave his palace at once.

So the poor girl left her home and went away till she came to a river with rushes growing along the banks. She gathered several armfuls and made herself a sort of rush cape with a hood, that hid her clothes.

After many days she arrived at a large castle. "Do you want a maid?" she asked the sentry. The sentry took her to the cook.

"Can you wash pots and scrub pans?" said the cook. The girl nodded her head. "Very well," said the cook. "What's your name?" But the girl wouldn't tell. "All right, we'll call you 'Cap o'Rushes'."

So Cap o'Rushes she became, and she stayed in the kitchen, scrubbing the pots and pans.

One day, there was to be a ball at the castle and all the maids were allowed to go to watch the dancing. But when evening came, Cap o'Rushes said she was tired and wanted to go to bed.

After the others had gone she took off her rush cape, washed herself, and went upstairs to the hall. There she danced every dance with her master's son, who fell in love with her the moment he saw her. After each dance he asked her name and where she had come from. But she refused to tell him. Then he gave her his ring, saying that he must see her again or he would die.

Before the ball was over, Cap o'Rushes slipped away and was in bed when the other maids came in.

Her master's son inquired far and wide for the lovely lady he had danced with. But nobody knew who she was. He grew pale and thin, and eventually took to his bed, and refused to eat.

One day, Cap o'Rushes said to the cook, "Let me make some soup for the young master." The cook agreed, and Cap o'Rushes made a delicious-smelling soup. But before it was carried upstairs she secretly dropped the ring into the bowl.

Because the soup smelt so good, the young man couldn't resist eating it. And imagine his surprise when he saw his ring at the bottom of the bowl! He immediately sent for the cook and demanded who had made the soup.

"I did," whispered the cook.

"No, you didn't," said the young man. "Tell me who made this soup."

"It was Cap o'Rushes," said the cook.

"Send Cap o'Rushes to me," he ordered.

When Cap o'Rushes stood before him, he said, "Who are you, and where did you get this ring?"

"I'll show you," she said. She took off her rush cape and stood before him in her beautiful clothes.

Well, her master's son got better pretty quickly after that. And soon it was announced that he and Cap o'Rushes were to be married.

A grand wedding was prepared and everybody was invited, including the king, Cap o'Rushes' own father. But she still told no one who she was.

Before the wedding, Cap o'Rushes went to the cook. "I want all the food that is presented to the king to be cooked without salt," she said.

"Very well," said the cook. "But he won't like it."

At last the great day came and everybody sat down to the wedding feast. The whole company began to eat. Except the king. He tried dish after dish but nothing was to his liking. Suddenly he burst into tears!

"What *is* the matter?" asked the bridegroom.

"Oh!" said the king, "I had a daughter once, who told me she loved me as uncooked food loves salt. And I sent her away for I thought she didn't love me at all. Now I see she loved me best of all, but she may be dead by now!"

"No Father. Here she is," said Cap o'Rushes, putting her arms round him.

And then they were all happy.

# The Old Woman and her Pig

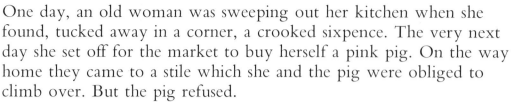

One day, an old woman was sweeping out her kitchen when she found, tucked away in a corner, a crooked sixpence. The very next day she set off for the market to buy herself a pink pig. On the way home they came to a stile which she and the pig were obliged to climb over. But the pig refused.

The old woman walked on a little way and met a dog. She said: "Dog, bite pig: pig won't climb over the stile and I shan't get home tonight." But the dog refused.

She walked a little further and met a big stick. She said: "Stick, beat dog: dog won't bite pig; pig won't climb over the stile and I shan't get home tonight." But the stick refused.

The old woman continued on her way and met a fire; and she said: "Fire, burn stick: stick won't beat dog; dog won't bite pig; pig won't climb over the stile and I shan't get home tonight." But the fire refused.

A little further down the road the old woman came to some water, and she said to the water: "Water, quench fire: fire won't burn stick; stick won't beat dog; dog won't bite pig; pig won't climb over the stile and I shan't get home tonight." But the water refused.

Standing near the water was an ox and the old woman turned to the ox and said: "Ox, drink water: water won't quench fire; fire won't burn stick; stick won't beat dog; dog won't bite pig; pig won't climb over the stile and I shan't get home tonight." But the ox refused.

The old woman walked on and met a butcher. She clasped her hands together and said: "Butcher, kill ox: ox won't drink water; water won't quench fire; fire won't burn stick; stick won't beat dog; dog won't bite pig; pig won't climb over the stile and I shan't get home tonight." But the butcher refused.

The old woman then spied a piece of rope hanging from a branch and she said: "Rope, hang butcher: butcher won't kill ox; ox won't drink water; water won't quench fire; fire won't burn stick; stick won't beat dog; dog won't bite pig; pig won't climb over the stile and I shan't get home tonight." But the rope refused.

Suddenly a rat ran past the old woman, and she called out to it: "Rat, gnaw rope: rope won't hang butcher; butcher won't kill ox; ox won't drink water; water won't quench fire; fire won't burn stick; stick won't beat dog; dog won't bite pig; pig won't climb over the stile and I shan't get home tonight." But the rat refused and ran on.

Under the hedge a cat lay sleeping. The old woman approached the cat, and pleaded with it: "Cat, kill rat; rat won't gnaw rope; rope won't hang butcher; butcher won't kill ox; ox won't drink water; water won't quench fire; fire won't burn stick; stick won't beat dog; dog won't bite pig; pig won't climb over the stile and I shan't get home tonight."

The cat listened carefully and when the old woman stopped, quite breathless, the cat looked at her slyly and said: "If you go over to that cow in the field and bring me back a saucer of milk I will kill the rat." The old woman hurried away to the cow and asked for a saucer of milk. The cow said: "I will give you a saucer of milk if you go over to the haystack and bring me back a handful of hay."

The old woman brought the cow the hay and in return the cow gave her a saucer of milk which she took to the cat. The cat drank the milk and then . . .

The cat began to kill the rat; the rat began to gnaw the rope; the rope began to hang the butcher; the butcher began to kill the ox; the ox began to drink the water; the water began to quench the fire; the fire began to burn the stick; the stick began to beat the dog; the dog began to bite the pig; the pig climbed over the stile and the old woman got home that night.

# Snowflake

A long time ago in Russia there lived a couple who longed for a child. But the years passed, and no child was born. One winter's day the wife was watching the village children at play in the snow.

"How I wish one of those children was mine," she sighed.

Youshko, her husband took her hand. "Look, Marusha," he said, "the children have made a snowman. Why don't *we* go out and make one too?" And he led her past the happy children to a patch of fresh snow hidden behind a clump of trees.

"Oh, Youshko, I feel like a little girl again!" laughed Marusha.

And they made a snowman, small as a new baby, first its body, then its head with little eyes, a mouth, ears and a tiny nose.

As she stood up and brushed the snow from her hands, Marusha looked at the little snow-child and blinked. For she saw two blue eyes gazing up at her, and not snow, but a white fur cap, not the glint of sunlight, but golden hair . . . As husband and wife stared, the snow-child became a baby girl.

She held up her arms to be picked up, and crowed with pleasure, and curled her fingers in Marusha's hair. They could hardly believe

this wasn't a dream. But they carried her home, gave her some supper and put her to bed. In the morning she was still there.

"We shall call her Snegorotchka, Snowflake, for she was made out of the snow," said Youshko.

Snowflake grew quickly, and soon she was joining the other children in their games in the snow, laughing and singing and throwing snowballs. And she showed them how to make beautiful snow castles, fountains and animals and to dance and whirl and drift like a snow-flake.

But at last the snow began to melt. Streams gurgled cheerfully through the forest again. The warm winds of spring woke the earliest flowers, a hazy green touched the trees, and the air was full of scents and bird song.

And Snowflake grew quieter. No longer did she join in the other children's games. She sat in the cottage, pale and sad, gazing out.

"Are you not well, my child?" asked Marusha.

"No, Little Mother," replied Snowflake. "My heart seems to turn to water when the warm wind blows."

"Why do you not go out to play, little one?" asked Youshko.

"I miss the snow, Little Father," said Snowflake.

"Come and look at the white cherry blossom. That is like a cloud of snow. Let us all go."

So they did, Snowflake walking between the old couple. But the child shuddered at the sight of the flowers, and the soft breeze set her trembling, so that Youshko put his arm round her to shield her.

Suddenly a shaft of sunlight pierced through the trees, and Snowflake cried out in pain. They turned to see tears running down her face. Sadly she turned sparkling eyes to them and, as they watched, she grew smaller and smaller, until there was nothing but a patch of damp grass and a single white flower where she had stood.

# Clever Gretel

Many years ago there was a young girl called Gretel. Now Gretel's main love in life was food and drink, so she went to work as a cook for a rich man who had a big house in the woods.

One day, the rich man asked her to prepare a special dinner for himself and a guest. Gretel decided to roast a couple of chickens, and early that evening she stoked up the fire and put two plump birds on a spit to roast above the flames. She had already prepared the other food and had laid the table, so she sat down with a mug of cider. After a while the chickens were cooked, so she told her master. But the guest had not arrived, and the rich man went out into the woods to search for him.

Now Gretel was getting hungry. The dinner smelled so delicious, she thought she would have a little taste of the chicken. She looked out of the window. No one was coming, so she cut off a chicken leg and ate it quickly. Then to make it look less obvious, she cut off the second leg.

Gretel licked her lips, but she was still hungry. A few moments later, she cut off the legs of the other chicken. And so it went on. Each time she cut a piece off one chicken, she had to match it with the other. So mouthful by mouthful, the two chickens were eaten.

Soon the rich man returned to say that his guest was just arriving. He asked Gretel for the carving knife so that he could sharpen it.

Meanwhile the visitor arrived. Gretel met him at the front door.

46

"Quick! You must run," she whispered. "My master is so angry with you for being late that he's sharpening his knife to cut off your ear."

The visitor did not need to be told twice. He turned and ran as fast as his legs would carry him.

Then Gretel went to her master and said, "Quick! You must run after your visitor. He has stolen the two chickens."

"What?" said the man. "BOTH of them! I'll get him for this."

Then brandishing the sharp knife, he ran after his visitor shouting, "I'll catch you for this. Both of them indeed! BOTH of them!"

The visitor thought he meant both his ears, so he ran even faster.

And Gretel pulled her chair closer to the fire and smiled.

# Puss in Boots

Once there was a miller who had three sons. When he died, he left the mill to his eldest son, a donkey to the second, but for the youngest son there was only a cat.

The poor lad was very disappointed. "What use is an old flea-bitten cat? Why there isn't even enough fur on him to make me a hat!"

Hearing this, the cat said, "Master, don't despair. If you get me a pair of fine boots and a sack, I will make your fortune."

The miller's son had nothing to lose, so he did as the cat said. The cat put on his fine new boots, slung the sack over his shoulder and strode off to a rabbit warren nearby. In no time at all, Puss in Boots (as he was now called) caught two rabbits. He threw them in the sack and went to the king's palace and asked to speak to the king.

"Your majesty," he said and gave a low bow, "I bring you these rabbits as a gift from my master, the Marquis of Carabas." The king was very pleased and told Puss to thank his master.

The next day Puss brought the king two pheasants, with the compliments of his master, and once again the king was pleased.

This continued until one day, Puss overheard that the king and his daughter, the beautiful princess, were planning to drive along the river in their carriage. Puss ran to his master and said, "Our time has come. Go quickly and bathe in the river and leave the rest to me." The miller's son wondered at the cat but did as he was told.

As the king and princess were driving near the river, they heard a cry. "Help! Help! My master, the Marquis of Carabas is drowning!" It was Puss in Boots. He told the king that thieves had stolen his master's clothes while he was bathing. (In fact, Puss had hidden them himself.) The king ordered his men to rescue the marquis from the river and to fetch him some clothes from the palace.

When the miller's son was dressed in royal clothes, he looked very handsome indeed. The princess fell in love with him instantly and persuaded her father to invite him to ride with them. The king thanked the marquis graciously for all the gifts his cat had brought.

Meanwhile, Puss in Boots ran ahead until he came to some haymakers in a field. He said to them, "The king is coming. If he asks you who owns these fields, you must answer that it is the Marquis of Carabas. If you do not , I will scratch your eyes out!" Then Puss ran on until he came to some woodcutters in a forest and he said the same thing to them. And he continued until he reached some fishermen by a lake and he also told them to say the same thing.

Finally, Puss reached the castle of an ogre who owned all the surrounding lands. Although he was quaking in his boots, Puss hailed the ogre boldly, "Greetings, sir, I have heard you have the amazing power to change yourself into a tiger. Surely, this can't be true?"

"Indeed, it is," replied the ogre and instantly turned himself into a ferocious tiger.

"That is truly remarkable," said Puss. "But, surely it is impossible for you to take the shape of a tiny mouse?"

The ogre snorted, "Why nothing could be easier," and he changed into a tiny mouse. In a split second Puss pounced on the mouse and swallowed him in one gulp. And that was the end of the ogre.

In the meantime, the king's carriage had reached the hay fields.
"Who owns these fields full of hay?" asked the king.
"The Marquis of Carabas!" the haymakers replied.
And the king's carriage drove on until it reached the forest.
"Who owns this forest full of straight timber?" asked the king.
"The Marquis of Carabas!" the woodcutters replied.
And the king's carriage drove on until it reached the lake.
"Who owns this lake full of fish?" asked the king.
"The Marquis of Carabas," the fishermen replied.

The king turned to the marquis and said, "I must congratulate you on your great wealth."

By this time the king's carriage had arrived at the ogre's castle. Puss in Boots greeted them at the gate saying, "Your majesty, welcome to the castle of my master, the Marquis of Carabas!" The king was amazed. The miller's son was even more amazed at his clever cat but he said nothing.

They entered the great hall and sat down to a magnificent feast. It was not long before the miller's son (now truly a marquis) asked to marry the princess and the king was only too glad to consent.

As for Puss in Boots, well, he was the guest of honour at their wedding and danced in his fine boots, of course. And he never chased mice again except for fun.

# Twelve Dancing Princesses

Once there was a king who had twelve beautiful daughters. The princesses were never apart, even at bedtime, when they went to sleep in twelve separate beds in the same room. The mysterious thing was, that every morning their satin slippers were worn to shreds as if they'd been dancing in them.

When the king asked his daughters what they'd been doing, they replied that they'd been asleep. And indeed, when he listened at their door during the night, all was still. So the king began locking his daughters in every night, but still their slippers were full of holes. The king could find no explanation, so he issued a proclamation that if any man could discover how the princesses wore out their shoes every night, he could marry the princess of his choice.

Princes from all over the land came to the palace to try their luck. One by one they spent the night outside the princesses' bedroom, listening and watching for any movement, but by morning each prince had disappeared, never to be seen again.

Not far from the palace lived a young goatherd called Michael. When he heard the king's proclamation, he too wanted to try to solve the mystery. But he knew that because he wasn't a prince, he would never be allowed to take his chance. So he went to the palace and was taken on as the gardener's boy.

Every morning Michael was to give each·princess a bouquet of her favourite flowers, freshly picked from the garden. The first morning, when he presented the flowers, not one of the princesses bothered to look at him except the youngest one. When she gazed at him with her lovely eyes, he fell instantly in love. She, too, thought he was very handsome but dared not say so as he was a mere gardener's boy.

That night when the princess went to bed, Michael put on a cloak
which made him invisible and crept up behind them into their room.
But instead of getting ready for bed, the princesses put on their finest
jewels, ballgowns and satin slippers.

Then the eldest princess opened a trap door and the princesses
began to walk down a secret staircase. Michael followed behind the
youngest princess, but he was too close and he stepped on her dress.

"Oh, someone's stepped on my dress!" she cried.

"Look behind you," said the eldest sister. "There's no one there."
And true enough, the youngest princess could see nothing because
Michael was invisible.

At the bottom of the stairs the eldest sister opened a door and the
princesses entered a forest where all the leaves were made of beaten
silver. Next they walked through another forest where the leaves
were made of beaten gold and finally through a third forest where the
leaves glittered with diamonds.

Soon they reached a lake where twelve beautiful little boats lay waiting, with a prince in each one. Each princess stepped into a boat and the prince rowed her across to an island. Michael hopped into the boat with the youngest princess. Their boat was far behind all the others and the princess complained, "Why are you so slow?"

"I can't understand it," said the prince who was rowing. "The boat seems so heavy tonight."

When they reached the island, a grand ball was already in progress. Musicians played in a pavilion and the princesses danced with their partners on the lawn. Lanterns blazed and there were fireworks in the sky. Michael stood back so that none of the dancers would bump into him and watched. Oh, how he longed to dance with his princess.

The ball went on until dawn and Michael could see that the princesses' slippers were worn to shreds. The instant the cock crowed, the musicians and dancers stopped completely.

"Hurry up!" cried the eldest princess, "Get the wine. The princes must drink it or else the enchantment will be broken." A cup of wine was passed round and all the princes took a drink. No sooner were they finished than the cock crowed a second time. The sisters got into the boats and the princes rowed them across. They waved goodbye to each other and the sisters hurried off through the forest with leaves glittering with diamonds, through the forest with golden leaves and last of all through the forest of silver leaves. Just before they left the last forest, Michael snapped off a twig from a silver tree.

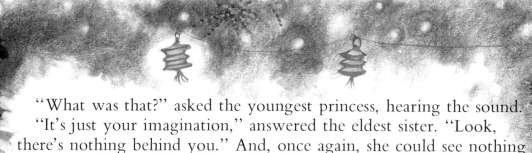

"What was that?" asked the youngest princess, hearing the sound.

"It's just your imagination," answered the eldest sister. "Look, there's nothing behind you." And, once again, she could see nothing because Michael was invisible.

Just as they reached the door to the castle, the cock crowed for the third time. The sisters ran up the stairs, through the trap door and went to bed. Michael had to go straight to work in the gardens.

The princesses woke at noon and when they came down to the garden, the gardener's boy presented them each with a bouquet. In the centre of the flowers for the youngest princess, Michael had placed the twig with silver leaves. When she saw the silver twig, she was so stunned she could say nothing.

The same thing happened again on the second night. Wearing his invisible cloak, Michael followed the twelve sisters through the three magical forests to the lake. Once again he crossed the lake in the boat with the youngest sister and watched the twelve princesses dance all night until their slippers were in tatters.

When the cock crowed, the princes drank the enchanted wine and the princesses hurried home. This time Michael picked a twig with golden leaves. Once again the youngest princess heard it snap but still she could see nothing.

"How jumpy you are," said the eldest sister. "Hurry up! It's nearly dawn."

That morning the gardener's boy presented the youngest princess with a bouquet containing the twig of golden leaves. The princess went pale with fright but still said nothing.

On the third night Michael followed the twelve princesses, yet again, but this time he brought back a twig with diamond-spangled leaves which he put in the youngest sister's bouquet.

When she saw it, she could control her curiosity no longer. "Boy, how have you discovered our secret?" she asked.

"By following you for the past three nights," replied Michael. "And when I tell your secret to your father, I will be entitled to choose one of you for my wife."

"Don't be impudent," snapped the princess. "A mere gardener's boy can't marry a princess," and she walked off.

But Michael was not discouraged. He found some elegant clothes

then asked the king to allow him to try to discover the secret.

That night he followed the twelve princesses through the three enchanted forests to the lake but this time he was not invisible. They welcomed him, thinking he was another dance partner, and no one recognized him as the gardener's boy, except the youngest.

Michael danced all night with one princess after another. When the cock crowed and the wine was brought, the eldest princess offered him the cup.

"If you drink, you will never grow old or die," she said. "You will dance and feast for evermore."

"If I drink, I will become enchanted like the others and be nothing but an empty shell," said Michael. "But if I don't drink, you," and he looked hard at the youngest princess, "must marry a gardener's boy. What shall I do?"

The youngest princess turned away, but just as Michael raised the cup to his lips, she cried out, "Don't drink! I will marry you, even if you are only a gardener's boy."

Michael leapt up to give her a kiss and in doing so dropped the cup. Instantly, the spell was broken.

The princes awoke as if from a dream and came back with Michael and the twelve princesses to the castle. Michael told the king how his daughters had worn out their satin slippers, night after night. When the king asked Michael to choose which princess he would marry, he naturally chose the youngest one. But she did not become the gardener's wife after all because the king made Michael a prince.

# How a Fish Swam in Air

Mr Moonbucket was a happy man as long as his gossip of a wife was not getting him into trouble with the neighbours.

One day, he was out cutting wood when his foot suddenly sank into the earth.

"What have you found, foot, I wonder?" he said. And he dug down, till he found a clay jug full of gold pieces. "Oh dear! When my wife finds out, she'll tell everyone, and there'll be trouble!" Then he had an idea. He walked the three miles to the nearest town and bought a live pike and a live hare in the market. When he was nearly home, he hung the pike high up in a tree and put the hare in a net, which he pegged under the bank of a stream.

Then as fast as he could, he ran home.

"Wife, wife!" he cried. "Come quickly! I've found a pot of gold! But you must never talk of it."

"Where is it, then?" she asked.

"In the forest. It's too heavy for me to bring back alone," he said.

On the way, Mr Moonbucket stopped suddenly. "I hear fish are living in trees now," he told his wife. "And wild animals are living in water!"

"What nonsense you talk, Moonbucket!" she said.

"What is that then?" said her husband, pointing to the top of a tall beech tree.

"The times are changing after all," gasped Mrs Moonbucket. "It's a pike! Well! A fish is a fish. Fetch it down for supper!"

Further on they heard a splashing in the stream:

"There's something in my net!" exclaimed Mr Moonbucket. "Look, wife, it's a hare!" But the hare was too quick. It wriggled out of his grasp and lolloped away.

"I wouldn't have believed it!" said Mrs Moonbucket. "But you let a good dinner escape with your clumsiness." And she boxed Mr Moonbucket's ears.

Then together they carried the jug of gold home. And from then on they lived very comfortably. But Mrs Moonbucket spent far too much money feasting her friends.

"You are wasting our gold," her husband complained. "You shall have not a penny more!"

"So!!" Mrs Moonbucket was very angry. As soon as her husband left the house, off she went to complain to the baron.

"He keeps the gold all to himself, and he won't work," she began.

"Gold?" The greedy baron's eyes glittered.

"The treasure we found – "

"I'll come at once!" said the baron. And he went with Mrs Moonbucket to see her husband.

"I'm afraid I'll have to look after that gold, my friend," he told Mr Moonbucket. "Buried treasure belongs to the king!"

"What treasure?" Mr Moonbucket asked.

"You'll be beheaded if you don't hand it over," warned the baron.

"But what treasure? My lord, let my wife tell you how we found it. Then you'll see what nonsense she talks," said Mr Moonbucket.

"Well," Mrs Moonbucket began, "we walked along the forest path, and first we found a pike at the top of a tree."

"A pike in a tree? Never!" smiled the baron.

"It was odd, yes. Then we fished a live hare out of the stream. It did splash!" Mrs Moonbucket went on.

"Ha-ha-ha!!" roared the baron. "That'll teach me to listen to a gossip. And after the hare, you found the buried treasure. Ha-ha-ha!" He was so pleased with her story that he told it at a banquet to all his friends. And soon after the whole village had heard it. And whenever Mrs Moonbucket started to gossip, her laughing neighbours would say:

"A pike in a tree! A hare in the stream! Ha-ha-ha!!"

So Mrs Moonbucket was cured of gossip, Mr Moonbucket bought a shop in the town, and they lived happily for the rest of their lives.

# The Elves and the Shoemaker

There was once a shoemaker who had fallen on hard times. The day came when he had enough leather for only one more pair of shoes. It was beautiful red leather, and before he went to bed that night the shoemaker cut it with extra care and laid it out on his bench ready to sew the next day. Then he and his wife climbed the winding stairs to their bedroom, said their prayers, and fell asleep.

The following morning when he came downstairs, the shoemaker was amazed to see the red shoes lying finished on his workbench. He examined them carefully and was forced to admit that never in his life had he seen a pair of shoes made more beautifully than these.

Later that day, a nobleman, passing through the town, called on the shoemaker, and when he saw the red shoes he immediately insisted on trying them on. They fitted perfectly and he paid much more than the usual price for them. Now the shoemaker had enough money to buy leather for two pairs of shoes.

He cut these out in the evening, and the next morning there they lay on the workbench, beautifully sewn and polished, and just waiting for a customer. Soon these shoes, too, had been sold. And now the shoemaker had enough money to buy leather for four pairs of shoes!

Again he found the shoes finished and waiting for him in the morning. And so it continued. Whatever the shoemaker cut out one day was always finished and waiting for him the next morning.

His fame began to spread. Customers came from far and wide. For his shoes were declared to be the most comfortable, the most stylish and the most beautifully made of any shoemaker in the land. And far from being poor, he became rich.

One evening his wife said to him: "Let us sit up tonight and see who it is that has brought us such good fortune."

So, instead of going upstairs to bed, they crouched behind the settle to see what would happen.

Around midnight two little men came into the room. They immediately took up the leather and hammered and stitched with their tiny fingers. In no time, they had finished one pair of shoes: the shoemaker could hardly believe his eyes. They straightaway started on another pair and never stopped working until they had finished all the work that was lying on the bench. Then they ran away.

The shoemaker and his wife came out from behind the settle, stiff with crouching so long. His wife said: "These little men have changed our lives. We must thank them. I will make some clothes: they have so little. And you shall make them a pair of shoes apiece." The shoemaker gladly agreed, and all that day he and his wife cut and stitched, so that by evening two little jerkins, two pairs of breeches, two pairs of stockings, two red knitted hats and two pairs of fine pointed shoes lay waiting.

Again, the shoemaker and his wife hid themselves. And again the little men appeared. When they saw the lovely clothes, they hugged each other in delight. They tried them on, and hopped and danced about the room with glee. Then they ran off.

The shoemaker and his wife looked at each other and asked: "Will they come again tomorrow night?"

But the little men never came back. As for the shoemaker, he became more and more famous. He made shoes for all the lords and ladies in the land, and even the king, when he wanted an extra special pair of shoes, would send for the shoemaker and ask him to make them.

# Dinewan and Goomblegubbon

Long ago, in Australia, the leader of the birds was Dinewan, the emu. Goomblegubbon, the turkey, watched the emu soaring gracefully overhead on her wide, strong wings and she turned to her husband.

"Look at Dinewan," she gobbled. "What right has she to keep an eye on us just because she is the largest? I am far cleverer than she – and what's more I am going to prove it!"

The next day, Goomblegubbon, the turkey, heard a whoosh of wings overhead. Dinewan was about to land. By the time the cloud of dust had settled, the turkey was sitting with her wings tucked completely out of sight.

"Why, how nice to see you, dear Dinewan," said Goomblegubbon. "Isn't it a beautiful morning?"

"You seem very happy today," said the emu.

"Well, life has been so much more pleasant since I got rid of my wings," smiled the turkey.

"Got rid of your wings?" screeched the emu, craning her long neck to each side to see for herself. "But why?"

"Wings are so common," said the turkey smoothly. "All the birds fly. But when they see how easy my life is, with no take-offs and

60

landings, they will say, "Let the wise Goomblegubbon be our ruler!"

Dinewan was dismayed to hear this. Of course flying was commonplace – why had she never noticed before? She spoke to her husband about it.

"Don't worry," he said. "We can outwit that old turkey. Shut your eyes and I'll chop off your wings. Then you can still be ruler."

So the emu stood still while her husband chopped off her fine wings. Dinewan raced off unsteadily on her spindly legs to find Goomblegubbon, who was sitting where she had left her, with her wings still hidden.

"You will never be ruler of the birds," she said, "because now, I, too, have no wings. My dear husband has chopped them off."

"Then more fool he!" cackled the turkey, and she unfolded her wings from her sides and flew away over the emu's head.

Of course Dinewan was furious and began to think up a scheme to trick Goomblegubbon. The next hot day, she left twelve of her fourteen children in their cool hut with her husband. Taking the two largest chicks with her, she set off to where the turkey was scrabbling for food with her large brood.

"What a surprise!" said Dinewan. "My two dear children and I are strolling along looking for titbits. It must be so difficult keeping your fourteen chicks well-fed. I suppose that's why they look a little scraggy."

"Scraggy!" squawked the turkey.

"Oh I know it's not your fault," went on the emu. "I am sure, my dear, that if you only had two you could give them so much food they would be almost as big as emus. Come chicks, supper time."

Goomblegubbon decided there was only one thing to be done. She took the little hammer she used for breaking snail shells and she knocked twelve of her children on the head. Then she hurried off with the two remaining chicks to where Dinewan was resting outside her hut.

"Look Dinewan, she called, "Now I have only two chicks, and they will soon grow to be twice the size of yours!"

"You wicked bird!" exclaimed the emu. "I wouldn't harm one of my chicks by so much as a feather!" And she called to her children and they all came running out in a bunch.

Goomblegubbon hung her head in shame, but it was too late, and to this day, the emu has no wings and many children, and the turkey has wings and only two chicks.

# Prunella

There once was a little girl who had to pass an orchard on her way to school. Every day she would pick a plum to eat with her lunch. And so she was called Prunella.

But the orchard belonged to a witch and one day, the witch caught Prunella picking a plum.

"You wicked child," she cried. "You'll live to regret stealing from me!"

"Oh, please forgive me," begged Prunella. "I didn't know the fruit belonged to you."

But the witch had no pity and took Prunella to her house and kept her prisoner for many years.

When Prunella was eighteen, the witch gave her a sieve. "Take this and fetch me some water from the well," she said. "If you do not, I will roast you alive."

Prunella took the sieve and scooped up some water from the well, but it ran straight through. Again and again this happened, until Prunella wept with despair.

Suddenly she heard a voice say, "Prunella, don't weep. I'll help you." There behind her stood a handsome young man. "My name is Bensiabel and I am the witch's nephew. I'll fill the sieve for you, but first you must give me a kiss."

"I won't!" cried Prunella. "I won't kiss the witch's nephew."

"Never mind," said Bensiabel. "I'll help you anyway." And he dipped the sieve in the well and the water stayed in.

The witch flew into a rage. "You may think you're clever, Prunella, but I'll get you in the end!" she cried.

The next day the witch gave the girl a sack of wheat and said, "Take this and bake me a loaf of bread. If it's not ready in one hour, I will roast you alive."

Prunella took the wheat and started to grind it into flour, but when she realized that she could never bake the bread in time, she wept.

Suddenly she heard Bensiabel saying, "Prunella, don't cry. I'll help you, only give me a kiss."

"Never!" cried Prunella.

"Never mind," said Bensiabel, and he took the wheat and in no time the bread was ready.

The witch was furious. "I'll get you in the end, Prunella!" she cried. "Tomorrow you will go to my sister's house to fetch a casket."

Prunella set off quite cheerfully. But on the way she met Bensiabel.

"Beware, Prunella!" he said. "The witch's sister means to kill you. But if you kiss me, I will save you." But Prunella refused.

"I won't," cried Prunella.

"Never mind," sighed Bensiabel. "I love you too much to see you die. Take this oil, this sausage and this rope and do as I say. At the witch's house, oil the door hinges; throw the sausage to the dog; and give the rope to the poor woman using her hair to pull up a bucket from the well. Then take the casket and flee."

Prunella did just as Bensiabel said. As she was running off with the casket, the witch heard her and called to the woman at the well, "Catch the thief!"

But the woman replied, "I won't, for she gave me a rope to pull up the bucket while you made me use my hair."

So the witch cried to the dog to seize the girl.

But the dog replied, "I won't, for she gave me a sausage while you let me starve."

Finally the witch called to the door to lock the girl in.

But the door replied, "I won't, for she oiled my hinges while you left me rusty."

So Prunella escaped and returned with the casket.

The witch could stand it no longer. "Your time has come, Prunella," she said, and started to sharpen her knife.

"Help me, Bensiabel!" cried Prunella in despair.

And Bensiabel whispered through the keyhole, "Now will you give me a kiss?"

"No," she replied.

Bensiabel hesitated, hoping she would change her mind.

"Oh, save me! The witch is coming after me," Prunella pleaded.

Bensiabel rushed in and threw himself on the witch. She stumbled backwards, fell out of the window and died.

Prunella turned to Bensiabel and said, "Now I will kiss you, for you have saved my life." Soon they were married and happy at last.

# The Three Wishes

A long time ago there lived a woodman and his wife. Every day the woodman went into the forest to cut down trees to sell the wood to the rich folk. It was a hard life and the pair were very poor. One day as the woodman was working away he was just about to take down a large oak, when he heard a voice calling him. He looked all round and to his astonishment there was a pixie sitting on the stump of one of the trees.

"Spare the oak, the queen of the forest, and you shall have three wishes," he said.

The woodman was so surprised he immediately agreed, and the pixie vanished.

In a daze, the woodman seated himself on the same stump and dreamed of what he should wish for.

A fine house, that's for sure, not too big, not too little, but just right.

Enough money to keep him and his wife contented till the end of their days. And the third wish? Well, his wife could have that one.

Quickly he stacked his logs and branches, picked up his axe and set off for home.

When he reached home his wife was taking in the washing.

"Dinner not ready yet?" he said, for he was hungry.

"Nay, not for an hour or so," said his wife. "You're early today."

"Aye," he said. "Wait till I tell you what happened in the forest."

"Tell me at dinner," she said, bustling about.

Well, the woodman sat there, getting hungrier and hungrier. At length he sighed. "Oh, I wish I had a juicy fat sausage, right now."

Clatter! Clatter! Rustle! Rustle! Down the chimney fell a juicy fat sausage, right at the woodman's feet.

"What's this?" said his wife. Then the woodman told her all that had happened to him that day.

"You dolt! You idiot!" she screamed. "Do you mean to say you've wasted one wish already on a *sausage*! Why, we could have wished for a nice house, new clothes, a fine carriage. I never saw such a fool. I wish that sausage was at the end of your nose."

In a trice, that's where it was.

They looked at each other in horror. She pulled and he pulled. But the sausage stuck fast.

"What shall we do?" he moaned.

"It doesn't look too bad," said she, looking at him with her head on one side. "I think I could get used to it."

Then the woodman saw that there was only one possible thing to do and that was to use the third wish fast, before his wife used it first.

"I wish this sausage off my nose at once," he said, in a loud voice.

Well! There it lay in a dish on the table. And if they didn't have a nice house, or new clothes, or a fine carriage, at least they had a large fat juicy sausage for dinner.

# Little Red Hen and the Grains of Wheat

One fine morning Little Red Hen was scratching for food round the farmyard when she found some grains of wheat.

"Cluck, cluck, cluck," said Little Red Hen hungrily and was about to gobble them up when she stopped.

"Ah ha . ." she said to herself. "If I don't eat these grains I could plant them."

Carefully she picked up the grains of wheat and carried them off to show to her friends, the pig, the cat and the goose.

"Look what I've found," she said.

But they weren't at all interested. The pig just grunted, the cat closed her eyes and the goose turned away.

"Who will help me plant these grains of wheat?" asked Little Red Hen.

"Not I," grunted the pig.

"Not I," said the cat.

"Not I," honked the goose.

"Very well," said Little Red Hen. "I shall do it myself."

The sun shone and the rain fell and slowly, very slowly, little green shoots pushed their way through the black soil. Little Red Hen *was* pleased with herself.

When at last the wheat was tall and golden she knew it was ready for cutting.

"Who will help me cut the wheat?" she asked her friends.

"Not I," grunted the pig.

"Not I," said the cat.

"Not I," honked the goose.

"Very well," said Little Red Hen. "I shall do it myself."

It was very hard work but at last it was all cut down.

Little Red Hen picked up the stalks of wheat and proudly carried them into the farmyard to show her friends.

"Look," she said. "The wheat is ripe. It is ready to be ground into flour. Who will help me take it to the miller's?"

"Not I," grunted the pig.

"Not I," said the cat.

"Not I," honked the goose.

"Very well," said Little Red Hen. "I shall do it myself."

She carried the wheat through the village and up the hill to the miller who lived in the windmill.

"Will you grind my wheat?" asked Little Red Hen.

"Certainly," said the miller, and he ground it until it was as smooth as silk.

"Thank you very much," said Little Red Hen.

"Goodbye clever Little Red Hen," said the miller.

"The wheat is ground into flour," Little Red Hen told her friends. "Who will help me take it to the baker's to be made into bread?"

"Not I," grunted the pig.

"Not I," said the cat.

"Not I," honked the goose.

"Very well," said Little Red Hen. "I shall do it myself." And she picked up the bag of flour and carried it to the baker's shop.

"Will you bake my flour into bread?" asked Little Red Hen.

"Certainly," said the baker, and he baked her a golden, crusty loaf.

"Thank you very much," said Little Red Hen.

"Goodbye clever Little Red Hen," said the baker.

"Look what I've got," said Little Red Hen to her friends.

The pig grunted greedily.

The cat purred hungrily.

The goose honked noisily.

Little Red Hen smiled happily.

"Who will help me eat this lovely bread?" asked Little Red Hen.

"I will," said the pig.

"I will," said the cat.

"I will," said the goose.

"But this time I don't need any help," said Little Red Hen. "I can eat it myself."

And she did!

# Tom Thumb

A man and his wife were sitting at the fire one evening, when the wife said, "Our house is so quiet! If only we had a child to fill it with laughter. Even if it were tiny – no bigger than my thumb – I would be so happy!"

Soon afterwards, a child was born to the couple: a perfect little boy who was only as big as his mother's thumb. "My wish has been granted!" she cried, and they decided to call their son Tom Thumb.

Tom Thumb never grew any bigger, but he was so good-natured and nimble, that he was a great help to his parents.

One day his father was getting ready to go into the forest to chop wood.

"I wish I had someone to drive the cart," he said, as he harnessed the horse.

"I will do it, Father" cried Tom Thumb.

"You are much too small to handle the reins,' said his father, laughing.

"But I can sit in the horse's ear and call to him which way to go."

"Just once then – we'll give it a try," said his father. "Bring the cart along in an hour or so," and he set off with his axe.

When the time came, his mother lifted Tom Thumb up into the horse's ear. By calling out, "Gee up!" or "Whoa!" Tom Thumb could guide the horse along the road. As he was turning a corner, crying out, "Gee up!", two strangers were passing and heard him.

"Good gracious! There's a cart being driven, and that was the driver's voice, but where is he?" They decided to follow the cart to find out.

When they all reached Tom Thumb's father in the forest, he called out, "Lift me down, Father!"

When they saw Tom Thumb, the strangers were very excited. "If we took him to a fair and put him on show he would make our fortunes," they said to each other. They went up to Tom Thumb's

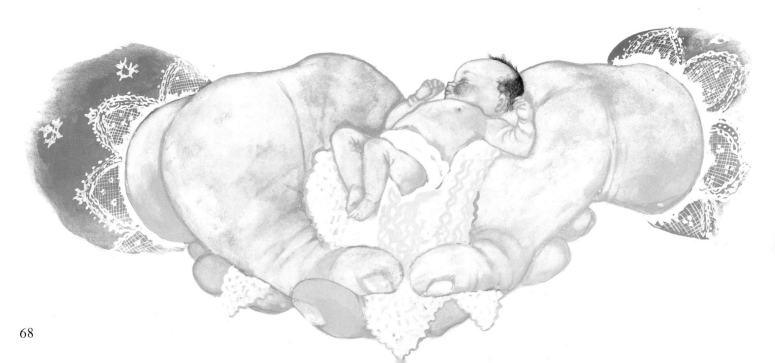

father and said that if he would sell them the child they would take the greatest care of him.

But the father refused: "I would not part with my son for all the gold in the world."

But Tom Thumb, who was sitting on his father's shoulder, whispered to him, "Sell me to them, Father. I am sure to return." So his father gave him to the men for a bag of gold.

One of the men put Tom Thumb on the brim of his hat, where he could watch the countryside as they walked along. When they stopped at dusk, Tom Thumb cried out, "Let me down now, I am quite dizzy."

The man put him on the ground, where he walked about slowly, as if stretching his legs. Then, quick as a flash, he darted into a mousehole. "Good evening, gentlemen," he called out. "You may go on your way without me now."

Although they tried poking sticks down the mousehole, it was too deep. Tom Thumb was safely round a corner. They went home without him or their money.

Later, Tom Thumb crept out. It was too dark to find his way home, but he came across an empty snail shell in which he curled up for the night.

He was just dropping off to sleep, when he heard voices saying, "The puzzle is, how exactly will we steal the merchant's gold?"

"I can tell you," interrupted Tom Thumb.

The thieves stopped in their tracks. "Who said that?"

"Lift me up and I will show you."

When they had found him, they lifted Tom Thumb up and he said, "Take me with you. I am so small, I can creep between the bars of the merchant's window and hand the gold out to you."

"A wonderful plan!" agreed the thieves, and they all travelled on together.

At the merchant's house, Tom Thumb crawled into the room. As soon as he was inside, he screamed with all his might, "Do you want everything that is here?"

The thieves were very alarmed and whispered, "Be quiet! Do you want to wake the whole household?"

But Tom Thumb seemed not to understand, for he called out again, "Just say which things you want me to steal!"

At this, the servant in the next room woke up and came running through. She lit a light and the thieves took to their heels and ran off unseen into the night. Tom Thumb had managed to slip through the window bars again, and settled down among the soft hay in the barn for a good night's rest.

At dawn the servant went to the barn to fetch some hay for the cow. She picked up the very armful in which Tom Thumb was sleeping peacefully. He didn't wake up until he was inside the cow's mouth.

It took him a moment or two to realize where he was, and then he dodged the teeth nimbly and slithered down into her stomach.

More and more hay arrived on top of him until he was quite squeezed into a corner and called out, "That's enough hay, thank you."

The servant turned pale with fright. Was the cow speaking to her? She rushed to her master and said, "Come quickly, the cow is speaking!"

"Don't be silly, girl," he said. And he came out to the barn in his dressing-gown.

He had just arrived when Tom Thumb called out again, "That's

enough hay, thank you – no more.''

The merchant decided the cow must be bewitched and the only thing to do was to have it killed. The cow's stomach ended up on a rubbish tip. Tom Thumb was just making his way out of it when a hungry wolf came along and swallowed it whole.

Even then Tom Thumb did not despair. ''Master wolf,'' he said, ''I know where you can find a fine feast.''

''And where might that be?'' asked the wolf.

Then Tom Thumb gave an exact description of his parents' house and how to find it. ''You can crawl into the pantry through the drain. There you will find bacon, sausages and whole hams hanging in rows – much more than you can eat.''

The wolf padded off at once and soon found the house. When night fell, he squeezed himself into the pantry and began to eat everything in sight.

The wolf was starting his second string of sausages when Tom began to shout and scream as loudly as he could. His parents woke up with a start and rushed to the pantry. Peering through a crack in the door, they saw the wolf. Tom's father went to fetch his axe.

''You wait outside the door,'' he said to his wife.

When Tom Thumb heard his father's voice, he called out, ''I am here Father!''

''It is our own dear son,'' cried his mother. ''Oh take care how you kill the wolf in case you harm Tom Thumb!''

So the husband knocked the wolf on the head and he fell down dead. Very gently they opened up its stomach and out sprang Tom Thumb, none the worse for wear.

''Where have you been?'' asked his parents.

''I have been in a mousehole, in a cow's stomach, and in a wolf's paunch. And now I am home to stay!''

His parents were overjoyed to see Tom Thumb again, and they never failed to laugh at the stories of his adventures.

# Little Red Riding Hood

Once upon a time there was a little girl who was called Little Red Riding Hood because she always wore a red velvet cape that her grandmother had made for her.

One day her mother said, "Little Red Riding Hood, today is your grandmother's birthday. Why don't you bake her a cake and take it to her as a surprise. She's been ill and it will help to cheer her up."

So Little Red Riding Hood baked a currant cake and packed it neatly in a basket with some other goodies for her grandmother. When she was ready to leave, her mother said to her, "Now make sure you go straight to your grandmother's house. Don't dawdle along the way or talk to strangers.'

"Yes, Mother," promised Little Red Riding Hood.

So Little Red Riding Hood set off through the woods, skipping and singing as she went. Soon she met a wolf, and oh, he was a handsome fellow.

The wolf gave her a big toothy smile and said, "Good morning, Little Red Riding Hood. Where are you going this fine morning?"

Little Red Riding Hood was so impressed by the friendliness of the wolf that she forgot all her mother's warnings.

"Good morning, Mr Wolf," she said politely. "I am going to my grandmother's house to give her a cake for her birthday."

Now, the wolf was very hungry and he thought to himself, "If I'm very clever I can gobble up both the little girl and her grandmother." So the wolf said to Little Red Riding Hood, "What a sweet girl you are. But why don't you take her a bunch of flowers too. I saw some lovely ones growing in the glade over there."

"What a good idea," said Little Red Riding Hood. "Thank you, Mr Wolf," and off she skipped in the direction the wolf had pointed.

Meanwhile the wolf hurried to the grandmother's house and knocked on the door.

"Who's there?" asked the old lady.

"It's Little Red Riding Hood," squeaked the wolf in a high voice.

"Oh, what a surprise! I'm too ill to get up, child, so lift up the latch and let yourself in."

The wolf lifted up the latch, opened the door, pounced on the old lady and gobbled her up in no time at all. Then he put on the old lady's clothes and crept into her bed.

By this time Little Red Riding Hood had gathered a huge bunch of flowers. Suddenly she realized how late she was and she hurried to her grandmother's house. She found the door wide open, so she went right in and over to the bed. She thought her granny looked very ill.

"Oh, Granny, what big eyes you have."

"The better to see you with, my dear," said the wolf.

"And Granny, what big ears you have."

"The better to hear you with, my dear," said the wolf.

"And Granny, what big teeth you have."

"The better to eat you with," said the wolf. And with that he sprang out of bed and swallowed poor Little Red Riding Hood in one gulp. Then he lay down to sleep on the bed.

That afternoon, a hunter passing by the cottage noticed that the door was open. "That's odd," he thought. "I'd better check that the old lady is all right."

When he entered the cottage and saw the wolf wearing the old lady's clothes asleep in the bed, he realized what had happened. He took his hunting knife and slit open the wolf's belly. Out popped Little Red Riding Hood and her grandmother completely unharmed. They were so grateful to the huntsman that they all sat down to celebrate with a piece of currant cake.

# Finn McCoull

Have you heard of Finn McCool? He was the Irish giant who began to build the Giant's Causeway from Ireland to Scotland. Finn was so big that he used a fir tree as a walking stick, striding up the Irish hills in a couple of paces.

But there was a giant who was even bigger than Finn. He was called Cucullin and it was rumoured he wanted to fight Finn to settle who was the stronger.

"Cucullin is so big, he is bound to beat me in a fight," said Finn to Oonagh, his wife. "Then I won't be able to hold my head up in Ireland again. I'll have to finish my causeway and escape to Scotland."

"Rubbish!" said his wife. "Just leave it to me."

Soon they heard Cucullin was on his way to pay them a visit.

"Off you go to all our neighbours," said Oonagh to Finn, "and borrow a dozen griddle irons."

When Finn arrived back he found Oonagh busily kneading dough. She took each griddle iron and put it in the middle of a flat, round loaf of bread, making a thirteenth loaf with no griddle iron in it. Finn couldn't see how doing a batch of baking was going to help him.

When the loaves were baked to a golden brown, Oonagh set them on the window ledge to cool. Looking out she saw the huge figure of Cucullin coming up the mountain.

"Quick!" she cried. "Put on this white shift, Finn, and get into the baby's cradle. Remember – you are the baby!"

Soon the door swung open and Cucullin bent down and came into the house.

"I am the great Cucullin, and I have come to show Finn McCool once and for all who is the strongest giant in Ireland," he boomed.

"Is that so! Well, just wait till I've finished sewing my husband's nightcap and I'll make you a cup of tea," said Oonagh, holding up a huge mattress case she was sewing.

Cucullin's eyes widened, but he said nothing.

"Now I'll put the kettle on. Oh, I forgot, Finn was going to crack open the rock behind the house for me. Our well has dried up, but he says there's a spring running there. As he's not here, could I ask you to do it for me?"

So Cucullin went outside, cracked the middle finger of his right hand three times, and split the rock so that water came gushing out.

"Thank you," said Oonagh, "but tell me, why did you crack the middle finger of your right hand three times like that?"

"Because that is where I keep my strength," said Cucullin, sitting down at the kitchen table and picking up the loaf which Oonagh had set before him. He spread it with half a churnful of butter and bit into it. Then he gave a great yell and clutched his jaw in both hands.

"Whatever is it?" asked Oonagh.

"You might well ask! I've only broken a couple of teeth on whatever it is!"

"Why, it's only the same bread I give to Finn and the baby," said Oonagh.

She took the thirteenth loaf, without the griddle iron in it, and handed it to Finn in the cradle, who ate up every crumb.

Cucullin was beginning to be thankful that Finn McCool was not at home. "I think I'll be off now," he said. "I'll just say goodbye to the baby."

"Show the man your fine white teeth, dear," said Oonagh to Finn, who opened his mouth obligingly.

"Just feel how sharp they are – especially the ones at the back," said Oonagh.

Cucullun put his right hand in and – snap! – when he pulled it out his middle finger was gone.

"Bad boy! I told you to wait till supper time!" scolded Oonagh. "Say sorry now."

But Cucullin had already gone. And they never saw or heard of him again.

# The Gingerbread Boy

Once there was an old woman who had no children but had always longed for one. One day, as she was baking gingerbread biscuits, she said to her husband, "I have a wonderful idea. I'm going to make myself a little boy out of gingerbread." And so she did.

She kneaded the dough and rolled it out, then she cut out a biscuit in the shape of a boy. She used raisins to give him eyes, a nose, a mouth and buttons on his coat. Then she popped him into the oven to bake. Soon she could smell that the gingerbread was ready and she opened the oven. No sooner had she done so than the gingerbread boy leapt out of the oven and ran out the kitchen door, shouting,

"Run, run as fast as you can.

You can't catch me, I'm the gingerbread man!"

Well, you can imagine, the old woman did not want to lose her precious gingerbread boy, so she called her husband and they both chased after the gingerbread boy. But they were too old and couldn't catch him.

The gingerbread boy ran down the road as fast as he could and soon he passed a pig sty. When the pig saw him he grunted, "Stop! Stop! little gingerbread boy, let me gobble you up!"

But the gingerbread boy ran faster and shouted,

"Run, run as fast as you can!

You can't catch me, I'm the gingerbread man!"

So the pig joined the old woman and her husband and chased after the gingerbread boy. But he was too fat and couldn't catch him either.

Soon the boy ran past a cow grazing in a field. When she saw him she mooed, "Stop! Stop! little gingerbread boy, let me gobble you up!"

But the gingerbread boy ran even faster and shouted,
"Run, run as fast as you can,
You can't catch me, I'm the gingerbread man!"

So the cow joined the old woman and her husband and the pig and chased after the gingerbread boy. But she was too slow and couldn't catch him either.

A bit further down the road the gingerbread boy passed a horse drinking water from a trough. When he saw him he neighed, "Stop! Stop! little gingerbread boy, let me gobble you up!"

But the gingerbread boy ran faster still and shouted,
"Run, run as fast as you can,
You can't catch me, I'm the gingerbread man."

So the horse joined the old woman and her husband and the pig and the cow and chased after the gingerbread boy. But he couldn't catch him either.

The gingerbread boy ran and ran until he came to a river and then he had to stop. How could he get across? Just then he saw a fox and he cried, "Fox, fox, can you help me to get across the river?"

Now the fox was a clever fellow and although he too wanted to gobble up the gingerbread boy, he did not say so. Instead, he said, "Hop onto my back then." And the little gingerbread boy did, and the fox began to swim.

When they were about halfway across the fox said, "Climb onto my head so that you don't get wet." And the gingerbread boy did.

The fox swam a bit further and then said, "Jump onto the tip of my nose so you can see the other side. But just as the boy reached the tip of the fox's nose, the fox threw back his head and gobbled up the gingerbread boy in one gulp. And that was the end of the little gingerbread boy.

## The Sleeping Beauty

Once upon a time, there lived a king and queen who dearly longed to have a child. When at last a daughter was born to them, they invited all the fairies in their kingdom to her christening.

Twelve fairies had been asked, but as they went in to the feast, a thirteenth arrived – an old fairy whom no one had seen for many years. Only twelve golden plates had been made for the occasion, so the old dame was hastily found a silver one. She muttered angrily through clenched teeth as she sat down.

Then the fairies came forward to offer their gifts to the baby princess. One gave her wisdom, the second a kind heart, the third beauty, the fourth a beautiful voice, the fifth grace of movement, and so on, until suddenly the uninvited fairy pushed her way past them all.

"When she is fifteen," she croaked spitefully, "she will prick her finger on a spindle, and die!"

But one more fairy had yet to speak. Now she said,

"I cannot undo this curse completely, but the princess will not die. She will only fall asleep for a hundred years."

Horrified, the king gave orders that every spindle and spinning-wheel in the kingdom was to be burnt.

The princess grew up to be a beautiful and kind-natured girl. Everyone was fond of her; she danced and played music beautifully, sang sweetly, and had all the other gifts the fairies had promised.

One day, shortly after her fifteenth birthday, she was wandering through the castle, exploring its passages, its nooks and crannies. At last she came to a narrow winding staircase in a tall turret; right at the top was a door. When she opened it, the princess was surprised to see an old woman, working busily at a whirring spinning-wheel.

"What are you doing, good dame?" she asked.

"I'm spinning a thread," replied the wicked old fairy, for it was she.

"May I try?" the princess begged.

"Certainly, my dear," said the fairy, with a sly smile.

As the princess touched the spindle, she pricked her finger. Next moment she slid gently to the floor and lay in a deep sleep. At the same time, everyone else in the palace, wherever they were, fell asleep too – the king and queen on their thrones, ladies-in-waiting and gentlemen of the court in the middle of their tasks, men-at-arms, leaning on their halberds, the cook sprawled across the pastry she was rolling out, grooms and horses in the stables, cats and dogs in the yard – all slept.

A thick forest of trees, brambles and briers sprang up around the castle. Soon it was so high that only the tips of the highest turrets could be seen.

Time passed, and a brave youth or two, hearing tales of a beautiful princess asleep in the castle, tried to force a way through the thicket; but not one succeeded. A hundred years had almost passed, when one day a handsome young prince came riding by and saw the towers in the distance. He had been told the tale of the sleeping beauty, and boldly he went forward.

As the prince drew near, the briers parted to let him through. Slowly he approached the castle. He passed the sleeping people, the sleeping animals in the courtyard, he wandered through the silent rooms, and at last reached the turret room. There lay the sleeping princess, and as a gentle breeze blew a strand of hair across her beautiful face, the prince knelt down and kissed her.

The princess awoke. She gazed up at the prince and smiled, and at that moment they both fell in love.

From all over the castle came the sounds of bustle and busyness as the entire royal household awoke too. Then hand in hand the happy princess and her prince went down to find the king and queen.

# Goldilocks and the Three Bears

Once upon a time there was a little girl called Goldilocks and she lived with her father and her mother in a house near a wood.

The wood was deep and dark and Goldilocks was not supposed to go into it alone, but one day when no one was looking, she decided that she would go exploring, so she opened the little wicket gate at the bottom of the garden and set off down the mossy path.

In the wood the trees were so tall and the leaves were so thick that Goldilocks could hardly see the blue sky above. Birds flew in and out of the branches, ivy covered the trunks, and primroses, celandines and wood anemones grew in little clumps at the roots. Catching sight of a bank of bluebells, Goldilocks started to pick a bunch of spring flowers for her mother, and she skipped happily down the path, gathering first one flower and then another, and all the while going deeper and deeper into the wood.

She was just about to turn round and go back home when the path widened and she found herself in a clearing. Straight ahead was a little house with lattice windows and a thatched roof. A wisp of smoke drifted from the chimney gently up between the trees.

"I wonder who lives in that dear little house?" thought Goldilocks. "I shall go and knock at the door and see."

So she went up to the front door and knocked on the little brass knocker, *rat-a-tat-tat*. Nobody came to answer the door so she knocked again. *Rat-a-tat-tat*. There was still no reply so Goldilocks went round to the window and, standing on tiptoe, she tried to peep in through the curtains. But it was no use, she was not tall enough.

"Perhaps the door is open," thought Goldilocks. "The people who live here will surely not mind if I sit down quietly and rest until they return."

So she went back to the door, lifted the latch, and let herself in.

Goldilocks found herself in a kitchen. The room was neat and clean. A fire burned briskly in the big black stove, and set upon the table were three bowls of porridge. There was a great big bowl, a medium-sized bowl, and a little tiny bowl. The porridge smelled so good and Goldilocks was so hungry after her long walk that she went over to the great big bowl and helped herself to a spoonful of porridge. But it was too hot. So Goldilocks tried a spoonful of porridge from the medium-sized bowl but it was too cold. So she tried a spoonful from the little tiny bowl and it was just right. In fact, it was so delicious that before she knew it, she'd eaten it all up.

Goldilocks was feeling a little tired and so she went to sit down. In front of the big black stove stood three chairs, a great big chair, a medium-sized chair and a little tiny chair. First of all, Goldilocks sat down in the great big chair. But it was too hard. Then she sat down in the medium-sized chair but it was too soft. So she sat down in the

little tiny chair and it was just right. But Goldilocks was too big for the little tiny chair and she broke it. She tumbled to the floor, the chair in splinters all around her.

"Oh dear, said Goldilocks, getting up carefully. "I wonder what there is upstairs?"

She went up a winding staircase and found herself in a pretty attic bedroom. In it there were three beds, a great big bed, a medium-sized bed and a little tiny bed.

"I do feel tired," yawned Goldilocks. "The people who live here will surely not mind if I have a little nap until they return." And she climbed into the great big bed. But it was too hard. So she climbed into the medium-sized bed, but it was too soft. So she climbed into the little tiny bed and it was just right. In fact, it was so comfortable that she instantly fell fast asleep.

By and by, down the mossy path and into the clearing, came three bears, tired and hungry and glad to be home. There was a great big Daddy Bear, a medium-sized Mummy Bear and a little tiny Baby Bear.

They opened the door of their little house and stepped into the kitchen. A delicious smell of porridge greeted them. They were just about to sit down and eat when the Daddy Bear growled,

"Somebody's been eating *my* porridge!"
And the Mummy Bear cried,

"Somebody's been eating *my* porridge!"
And the little Baby Bear squeaked,

"Somebody's been eating *my* porridge and they've eaten it all up!"
At that very moment they noticed the chairs.

"Somebody's been sitting in *my* chair!" growled the Daddy Bear.

"Somebody's been sitting in *my* chair!" cried the Mummy Bear.

And the little Baby Bear squeaked, "Somebody's been sitting in *my* chair, and they've broken it all to pieces!"

The three bears looked suspiciously around the room. The Daddy Bear went and looked in the cupboard, the Mummy Bear looked behind the stove and the little Baby Bear looked underneath the table. But there was nobody to be seen! So they went up the winding stairs to the bedroom.

What a disorder!

The Daddy Bear looked at the rumpled covers and growled, "Somebody's been sleeping in *my* bed!"

The Mummy Bear, seeing the dent in the pillow, cried, "Somebody's been sleeping in *my* bed!"

And the Baby Bear, peeping under his eiderdown, squeaked, "Somebody's been sleeping in *my* bed and they're still there!"

Goldilocks woke suddenly from a pleasant dream. With a start she saw three bears standing round her bed, staring at her angrily. Clasping her flowers, she ran to the window. She jumped straight out of it, down onto the ground. She picked herself up in a hurry and began to run down the mossy path. And, not daring to look behind her, she didn't stop running until she was safely home!

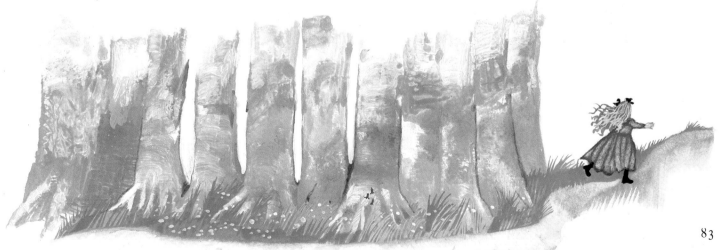

# The Emperor's New Clothes

Long ago there was an emperor who loved to wear beautiful clothes. One day two rascally weavers arrived at the palace and announced they could weave a marvellous cloth that was not only gorgeous to look at but also invisible to anyone who was stupid or could not do his job properly.

"With clothes made of this material I could find out who are the fools at my court," thought the emperor. So he gave the weavers a purse of gold and told them to begin work at once.

The two rogues locked the door, set up a loom without a single thread on the frame and did nothing at all.

The emperor was soon impatient to see how they were getting on, but he feared he might not be able to see the cloth. So he sent his prime minister.

"What do you think of it so far?" asked the weavers.

"Er – beautiful!" exclaimed the minister.

Then the rascals described the rich colours, the clever pattern and the minister repeated every word to the emperor. But he went home very worried.

"Am I stupid?" he asked himself. "For I saw nothing on the weavers' loom."

The weavers asked for more money, more silk and gold thread. They put all they were given in their knapsacks and pretended to work on.

Another minister was sent to inspect the material. He too could see nothing, but he too admired its excellence and praised it to the emperor.

At last the emperor thought it was time to go with all his court to see the marvellous cloth.

"Ah, what b-beautiful m-material!" the emperor stuttered, gazing in dismay at the empty loom.

"Beautiful INDEED!" cried the courtiers, staring at nothing. And they all agreed that the emperor must have robes made from the splendid cloth to wear in a special procession through the city. The emperor made the weavers Knights of the Dazzling Cloth and pinned medals on them. And they set to work with scissors and needles, snipping and sewing the empty air.

The emperor went to bed very worried. "Am I really stupid?" he wondered. "Unfit to be an emperor?"

In the morning the weavers announced that the Royal Robes were ready. They pretended to hold up the clothes. "Here are the coat, the trousers, the long train. Feel that! It's practically weightless."

The emperor undressed, and the rogues pretended to help him put on the invisible clothes.

"What colours! How magnificent!" cried the courtiers.

"The city awaits the procession!" boomed the master of the ceremonials. All the people had heard of their emperor's magical new clothes and had come out to admire.

Two fumbling chamberlains pretended to lift up the end of the royal train, and the emperor marched out proudly under his crimson canopy followed by his court.

"Hooray for the emperor! How beautiful! What style!" everybody shouted. For who would admit to being stupid?

"Why doesn't the emperor have any clothes on?" a small boy piped up suddenly, VERY LOUD.

"Hark at that child," laughed his father, embarrassed. But people began whispering:

"That child doesn't look stupid."

"So the emperor . . . the emperor . . . really doesn't have any clothes on!" And the crowd began to laugh.

Then the emperor realized he had been tricked. But he marched on through the delighted crowds looking prouder than ever.

# Rapunzel

Once upon a time there was a beautiful, young girl called Rapunzel. She had long golden hair and could sing like a bird. When Rapunzel was a child, a wicked witch had taken her from her parents. The witch kept Rapunzel at her house until she was twelve years old, then she locked her in a high tower with one small window at the very top, but no door below.

Each morning Rapunzel opened the window to sing and each morning the witch came with some bread and milk. On arriving, she called up to the window:

*"Rapunzel! Rapunzel!*
*Let down your hair."*

Then Rapunzel uncoiled her long hair, and the witch climbed up.

One day, a few years later, a prince was riding through the forest and heard Rapunzel singing. He was enchanted by her voice, and again and again he went back to the tower to listen.

Now one morning, while the prince was hiding in the bushes nearby, the witch arrived and he heard her say:

*"Rapunzel! Rapunzel!*
*Let down your hair."*

Then he watched in amazement as the witch climbed up the long golden hair.

The very next day as the sun went down, he decided to try the command himself.

*"Rapunzel! Rapunzel!*
*Let down your hair,"*

he called in a gruff voice, just like the witch's.

Rapunzel uncoiled her hair and in a few seconds the prince had climbed up to the window. At first Rapunzel was afraid. She had never seen a prince before. But he was kind and gentle and very handsome. After that the prince visited her every evening and soon Rapunzel loved him as much as he loved her.

But, alas, one morning Rapunzel said to the witch, "Why are you so rough when you climb up my hair? The *prince* never hurts me."

Immediately, the witch knew that Rapunzel had been tricking her. With three angry snips of her scissors she cut off the long, golden hair. And she sent Rapunzel to a far away land, where, she said, the prince would never find her.

That evening, when the prince arrived at the tower, the wicked witch let down Rapunzel's hair. Quickly the prince climbed up to the window to find to his horror – not Rapunzel, but the witch.

"You'll never see Rapunzel again," she screeched. She pushed him backwards and he fell into a bush of jagged thorns which blinded him in both eyes.

For many years the prince wandered from country to country Then one day, when he had almost given up all hope of finding Rapunzel, he heard her beautiful voice. With a cry of joy, he stumbled towards her. Rapunzel wept with happiness and two tears fell into the prince's eyes. At once he could see again.

Then the prince led Rapunzel to his own land where they were married and lived happily together for the rest of their lives.

# The Magic Porridge Pot

Once upon a time there was a little girl who lived all alone with her mother. They were very poor and the day came when there was nothing in the house for them to eat, not even a stale crust of bread. The little girl went out into the woods to search for nuts and berries, but she found nothing.

At last, tired and hungry, she flung herself down under a tree and wept. "What shall we do?" she sobbed. "Oh, what shall we do?"

Suddenly she felt a tap on her shoulder and heard a soft voice say, "Wipe your tears, little girl, I have something for you."

The little girl looked up and saw a small round woman wrapped in a black cloak.

"Who are you?" she asked, a little frightened.

"A friend," said the woman, smiling gently, and to the little girl's amazement she handed her a black cooking pot. She took it, then began to cry again.

"Thank you for the pot," she wept, "but it is no use to us . . . we have no food to put in it."

"This is a magic pot," said the woman. "Whenever you are hungry you must say to the pot – 'Cook, Pot, Cook!' And in no time at all you will have all the porridge you can eat. When you have enough you must say to the pot – 'Stop Pot, Stop!' and it will do as you command."

"Oh thank you, thank you," said the little girl. "I shall remember the magic words and we'll never be hungry again." And she ran off as fast as her legs would carry her to show her mother the magic pot.

After that the little girl and her mother were very happy, for they were never hungry. Then one sunny day the little girl went off by herself to the woods. She was away for a long time and the mother began to feel hungry.

"I'll make some porridge," she said. "I know what to do." And she went up to the pot and said, "Cook Pot, Cook!" Sure enough the pot was soon full of delicious creamy porridge. The mother took a big bowlful and started to eat . . . but then she noticed the magic pot was filling up again with porridge.

"Oh dear me," she cried. "Enough! Enough!" but those weren't the words the magic pot obeyed. The porridge reached the rim of the pot and spilled over the sides onto the table.

"No more, no more," yelled the mother, trying to remember the magic words. The porridge bubbled off the table and onto the floor,

it trickled out of the front door, down the steps, through the garden gate and down the hill. "Go away," shouted the mother running in front of it. "We don't want any more."

But the pot didn't obey. The porridge tumbled down the road like a great white river, it swirled round corners and flooded fields. It trickled under farmhouse doorways. It flowed thick and fast and strong through the village. And the mother ran on ahead waving her hands in the air and crying for help.

When the little girl came home from the woods, she could scarcely see her house for porridge.

"STOP POT, STOP!" she shouted as loudly as she could. And the little pot heard her, and it stopped.

And the people in the farms and villages for miles around brought out their buckets, bins, barrels and basins to scoop up the delicious, creamy porridge. There was enough for everyone – and for the dogs, the cats and the mice as well.

But never, never again did the mother forget the magic words . . . "Stop Pot, Stop!"

# The Wolf and the Seven Little Kids

Once upon a time there was an old nanny goat who had seven little kids. One morning she had to go to market, so she gathered her children round her and said, "I have to go out for the day so you will have to look after yourselves. Be sure not to open the door to anyone because it might be the wicked old wolf who will eat you all up. Remember, even if he tries to disguise himself, you can always recognize him by his black paws and gruff voice."

The little kids promised their mother they'd be careful and they bolted the door on the inside when she went out. Soon they heard a knock at the door.

"Open up, my darlings, it's your mother," said a husky voice.

But the little kids cried, "You can't fool us, you wicked old wolf! Our mother has a soft sweet voice and yours is gruff."

The wolf gnashed his teeth with anger and went away. When he got home, he swallowed a whole jar of honey to make his voice sweet. Soon he was back again, knocking on the goats' door.

"Open up, my darlings, it's your mother," said a sweet voice. But when the kids saw an enormous black paw on the window they cried, "You can't fool us, you wicked old wolf! Our mother has snowy white paws but yours are black as soot."

The wolf gnashed his teeth with anger and went away. When he got home, he dipped his paws in flour to make them white. Once

again he was back knocking on the goats' door.

"Open up, my darlings, it's your mother. I have a surprise for you."

The little kids heard the sweet voice and saw the white paws on the window and they opened the door. In sprang the wolf!

The little kids ran to hide as the wolf chased them about the house, snapping his teeth. One kid hid under the bed, another behind the bathtub, a third in the wardrobe, a fourth in the oven, a fifth on top of the cupboard, a sixth up the chimney and a seventh inside the grandfather clock. But the wolf soon found them and gobbled them up; all except the littlest kid who was hiding in the clock. The wolf was so full from eating the six little kids that he lay down on the bed and fell asleep.

When the old nanny goat came home, a dreadful sight met her eyes. The house was a shambles, with furniture overturned and crockery broken. She called each one of her kids by name but no one answered. But when she called the littlest one, a tiny voice cried out, "Mother, Mother, I'm hiding inside the clock." When she had helped him out, the little kid told his mother the terrible thing that had happened.

Suddenly they heard a loud snoring. There on the bed lay the wolf. The mother goat could see the kids wriggling inside the wolf's belly. She fetched a pair of scissors, and snip snip snip, she cut him open. One after another the little kids leapt out unharmed.

When their mother had given them each a hug, she said, "Now go and fetch me as many stones as you can carry." So they did. And the nanny goat stuffed them into the wolf's stomach and sewed it up.

When the wolf woke up he had a terrible stomach ache. He got up to get a drink of water and the stones were so heavy that he tumbled through the doorway and rolled down the hill straight into the river where he drowned.

# The Husband Who was to Mind the House

Once upon a time there was a bad-tempered man who thought his wife was lazy. Every day he would come home from the fields and shout and rage.

"I work my fingers to the bone," he would cry, "while you do nothing at home, except play with the baby."

"All right good husband," said the wife. "Tomorrow we'll have a change. I'll work in the fields and you can stay at home and look after the house and the child." And so it was agreed.

Early next day the wife picked up a scythe and waved goodbye to her husband and child. The man looked round the house.

"I'll churn the butter first," he thought. It was thirsty work he soon discovered, and besides, his arms ached. So, picking up the child, he went down to the cellar to draw a mug of cider.

Suddenly he heard a TRIT TROT TRIT TROT TRIT sound above. "Oh no!" cried the man. "That must be the pig. He will upset the butter churn." And he grabbed the child and ran up the cellar steps. Sure enough the pig *had* upset the butter churn, and a great pool of cream was spreading over the floor.

"Get out, pig," yelled the man. But as he was pushing it through the doorway, the child was crawling into the creamy pool.

There was no time to wash him, for next moment the man heard a splashing and a sploshing down in the cellar.

"Oh no!" he cried. And ran down the steps to find the cider barrel empty and cider swilling all over the floor.

"Bother the pig, and bother the cider," said the man crossly. And he started to make butter all over again. Then the cow started to moo.

"Oh no!" the man groaned. "I've forgotten to feed the cow! I've no time to take her to the meadow. What can I do?" He looked up and saw the thatched roof of his cottage. There was sweet grass growing through the straw.

"I'll put the cow on the roof," he thought. And he pushed and he pulled and he tugged until he had dragged the cow onto the roof.

Suddenly the child started to cry. "Oh no!" said the man. "I've forgotten to feed the baby."

He jumped off the roof, and ran into the kitchen to grind the oatmeal for the porridge. On the roof the cow mooed miserably.

"Maybe she is frightened of falling," thought the man. So he climbed onto the roof with a length of rope, tied one end round the cow and dropped the other down the chimney. Back in the kitchen he tied the rope round his ankle.

He was just putting the oatmeal into the pot which was heating over the fire, when the cow fell off the roof. As the cow fell down the man flew up the chimney, and there they were stuck, neither of them up nor down. And that's how the wife found them when she came home from the fields.

Quickly she cut the rope with her scythe. The cow dropped safely to the ground, but the man fell down the chimney head first into the pot of hot porridge.

"Shall I work in the fields today?" the wife asked next morning.

"Oh no, my love," said her husband sweetly. "I'll go out to work today." And he smiled happily as he kissed her goodbye.

And from that day to this, he never again complained that his wife was lazy.

## The Selfish Giant

There once was a wealthy Giant who lived in a handsome mansion surrounded by a splendid garden. Although he was rich, he was also very mean.

"If I go and stay for a time with the Cornish Ogre, I shall save a lot of money," he thought to himself one day. So he closed up his house, locked the big iron gates, and off he went. And he stayed with the Cornish Ogre for seven long years.

Meanwhile, the Giant's empty mansion grew cold and damp. The garden grew wilder and wilder and bit by bit the high garden wall crumbled.

The village children heard that the Giant was away, and soon his overgrown garden was their favourite place to play and climb, laugh and tumble. They particularly loved the orchard where, in Spring, twelve peach trees were covered in cheerful blossom, and in Autumn were weighed down with juicy fruit.

But at last the Giant came home. The children heard the squeal and scrape of the rusty gates and suddenly there was the angry Giant towering over them, waving his knobbly stick.

"What are you doing here?" he bellowed. "Get out of my garden." He rushed wildly at them, and they scattered and fled.

Then the Giant repaired his high wall, and put up notices all around. He was a very selfish giant.

But when Spring next came to the country, and everywhere was fresh and green, and the cuckoo was heard always in the distance, and swifts and swallows whirled about the sky, a strange thing happened. A little patch of Winter stayed on in the Giant's garden. Always there was a dark cloud overhead, the trees did not blossom, the daffodil and crocus shoots were nowhere to be seen and no birds sang. The windows of the Giant's mansion were always covered in frost, the north wind whistled through the corridors, and even knocked down some chimney-pots, and snow kept falling from the dark cloud. The selfish Giant shivered as he looked out at his white garden.

"This weather can't just go on and on," he said. But it did. The time for Summer came, and children played in the hot sun in the ripening golden fields. But no change came to the selfish Giant's garden: it just froze deeper and deeper.

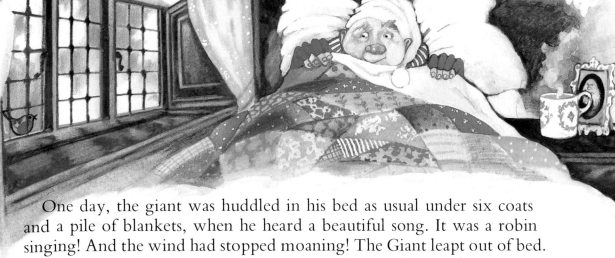

One day, the giant was huddled in his bed as usual under six coats and a pile of blankets, when he heard a beautiful song. It was a robin singing! And the wind had stopped moaning! The Giant leapt out of bed.

"It's Spring!" he cried, and threw open the window. What a surprise he had! Children had climbed into the garden and into nearly every peach tree in the orchard. And the snow was melting fast. Leaves and blossom were bursting out everywhere and the blue sky was alive with the whirring of wings.

There was only one small corner where it was still Winter and a single peach tree was covered in snow. A tiny child, too small to reach the lowest branch, was wandering round and round the tree.

"So that's why Spring wouldn't come," murmured the Giant. "Because I kept the children out. And now they've brought it back. I have been selfish. But never again!" he vowed to himself. He went down to the garden. But the children saw him, and ran away, and howling Winter returned again. Only the tiny boy did not escape. His eyes were so full of tears that he could hardly see.

Carefully the Giant lifted him up onto a branch. The tree burst at once into flower and leaf, and a blackbird came and sang on its topmost branch. When the other children saw that the Giant was not unkind any more, they came back. And the Spring came back with them.

"You can all come and play here whenever you like," said the Giant.

Then with a mighty sledge-hammer, he knocked down his great wall. And he pulled up his boards and notices, and made a bonfire of them. And all the children danced round the flames.

Every day after that, children played in the Giant's garden. And sometimes the Giant joined them in their games, though he was really too big and clumsy.

"Where is the very tiny boy?" he asked one day. "I don't think I've seen him but that once." But the children could not tell him.

Years went by, and the Giant grew old and feeble. Often he sat outside in a big old armchair and watched the children at play.

One mild evening, late in the year, he glanced at a corner of the peach orchard. He rubbed his old eyes, and looked again. One tree was in blossom there. It was covered in white blossom and at the same time hung with strange gold and silver fruit. The old Giant got up slowly and tottered towards it, leaning heavily on his stick. When he was closer, he recognized standing under the tree the same tiny child that he had lifted up into a peach tree all those years ago. He did not look one day older.

"I don't understand," the Giant whispered.

"You let me into your garden once," piped the child. "Today you must come to mine in Paradise." And he held out his hand.

Next day when the children came to play in the garden, they found their Giant lying at peace under a soft blanket of snowy blossom, a gentle smile on his lips.